AFTER THE INTERVIEW

by A.A. Abbott

A.A. Abbott

This book has been written by a British writer in British English.

Published by Perfect City Press.

ISBN 978-0-9929621-0-4

A WORD FROM THE AUTHOR

A special thank you to Ian, Tom and all the other family and friends who supported me in writing this book – they know who they are! Even bigger thanks to you for reading it. You're going to have fun! Sit back, relax and prepare to be entertained.

A.A. Abbott

BY AA ABBOTT

Up In Smoke

After The Interview

The Bride's Trail

The Vodka Trail

The Grass Trail

See https://aaabbott.co.uk for free short stories and more

Follow AA Abbott on Twitter @AAAbbottStories and on Facebook

Contents

Chapter 1 Boris: a big decision

Boris had been on edge all day. Now, he was sure from Melissa's face that his fears were about to be realised.

"I've got a question for you," she said, her brown eyes wide with excitement. Sitting opposite him in the candlelit restaurant, a strappy black dress revealing her figure, she'd never seemed more beautiful.

Boris took a sip of red wine, clutching the glass tightly to steady his hand. "Go on," he said, surrendering to the inevitable.

They'd lived together for over a decade. Each leap year, he'd breathed a sigh of relief when 29th February slipped past without incident. This time, he could practically hear the ticking of Melissa's body clock; a bomb about to explode, shattering the sweet life they shared.

It had been fun, a continuation of his student days but with considerably more money. On graduating, he'd found work with undemanding hours and reasonable pay, had bought in Greenwich at the right time and had plenty of credit to fund an active London social life. Melissa had been happy to move in. She'd decorated his flat, taking all the domestic duties upon herself. In the bedroom, she still beguiled him as much as on their first night together. He enjoyed showing her off in public, seeing friends and strangers envying him. All she'd appeared to want in return, at least until now, was simply to be supported in pursuing her passion for music.

"Will you marry me?"

"You're not pregnant, are you?" he asked.

Melissa's eyes lost their sparkle. "No. Why should that make any difference?" she challenged him. "Although it would be lovely to start a family, wouldn't it?"

Not for him, Boris thought.

"You haven't answered my question," Melissa said, her expression mulish.

"Darling, of course we'll get married. Yes, yes, yes." He smiled, hoping to hide his dread. However awful the notion of settling for a semi with garden and children, the thought of losing Melissa forever was even worse. There was no doubt she'd leave if he turned her down. He rose to his feet and bent to lift Melissa to hers, intending to hug her.

Waiters dashed to their side, asking if everything was all right. He wondered if they thought he intended to leave without paying.

Melissa was glowing. "Everything's perfect," she said "We just got engaged."

Then champagne would be on the house, they were told.

Melissa had booked an early table, and they left the restaurant in New Change shortly before nine o'clock. The waiters had a little difficulty finding Boris' overcoat – everyone in London seemed to wear a thick black wool coat in the middle of winter – but that was soon resolved.

"Just look for the smallest one," Melissa suggested.

Boris reddened.

"All the best things come in small packages," she whispered to him.

A few shops had late opening hours, their brightly lit windows dotted here and there among mostly shuttered premises. Melissa guided Boris inside a jewellers.

"There. That's the one I want." She pointed to a diamond ring glittering in a glass cabinet.

There were only two staff in the shop, a tall young man and an older woman, both briskly removing trays of jewellery from the window. "We're closed for the night. I've already cashed up," the woman said, barely glancing at them.

"We'll get it tomorrow, darling," Boris said. "Come along to the office at lunchtime, and we'll go to the shop together." He could see the stone was easily the largest on display, with a price tag to match. It would upset Melissa if he complained now. Tomorrow, he might change her mind. He smiled. "We need to make sure it's the right size, don't we? Or we could go to Hatton Garden if you like." He glared at the woman as he manoeuvred Melissa out of the shop.

"Hatton Garden? Is this one too expensive?"

"No, of course not. You can have any ring from any shop, anywhere. Just say the word and it will be yours."

He'd put it on the credit card, then worry about paying for it. Finding another job would be a good start. Perhaps someone at the squash club would have a lead. They were all accountants or lawyers and not short of cash. Idleness and inertia meant he'd stayed in his current role, one of the few in the City where it was acceptable to work nine to five. Moving would double his salary and not only give him enough to buy the ring, but also to cover the mortgage in a suburb of Melissa's choice. The bill for the wedding was another matter. Perhaps Melissa's father would dip his hand in his pocket, but Boris doubted it.

They strolled arm in arm to Bank, to take the Docklands Light Railway back to Greenwich. "Guess what? We're going to be married," Melissa told the late shift concierge at their apartment complex.

"Congratulations Miss Stevens, Mr Brooks," he said.

He was an Eastern European, a little older than Boris, and much taller, dark haired, ruddy and coarse-featured. A Pole or Slovak or some such. Boris had seen him before but couldn't recall his name. He peered at the man's badge. Szymon, that was it. No wonder it had slipped his mind. He had no idea how to say it, even.

Boris was sure the man was staring at Melissa's cleavage, and not for the first time. "Good night," he said stiffly, giving Szymon a filthy look, before putting an arm around Melissa's shoulders and heading to the lifts.

"Asshole. Shorty." Boris was sure he heard Szymon cursing. He turned round sharply.

"I beg your pardon. What did you say?"

"It's icy, surely?" said Szymon. He appeared to be suppressing a smirk. "I am sorry it was not clear. My English is not so good."

"Your English is fine, Szymon," said Melissa in an encouraging tone. She pronounced it as 'shy men'. "I wish I could speak Polish half as well."

Szymon flashed a grin at her.

Boris shook his head. She either hadn't heard Szymon swear, or had chosen to support the man's lie for some unfathomable reason.

"Remember who you're talking to, Szymon," he said.

He was still simmering when Melissa opened the door to their penthouse flat, hinting at her advance planning by telling him champagne was in the fridge.

"Of course he wasn't calling you names. You mustn't be so sensitive about your height," Melissa said, when they were ensconced in their living room overlooking the Thames. "Chin chin!" She topped up their glasses.

"You were confident I'd say yes, then?" Boris teased.

"I would have drowned my sorrows otherwise."

Her eyes suggested she would have packed a suitcase too. Nevertheless, his spirits lightened. He gulped the champagne, not caring if he went to work with a hangover the next morning, or even declared it a duvet day. His employers would soon be part of his history, along with, regrettably, his single status.

Chapter 2 Jed faces facts

Jed Gardner hadn't asked for coffee. The chief executive officer of GardNet didn't need to. It always appeared exactly when he wanted it.

Valerie placed his espresso in front of him and passed lattes to his visitors. Mark and Raj thanked her. Jed said nothing. He gulped the espresso and returned the empty cup to his PA's tray as she waited. She took it away, shutting his office door behind her.

Jed remained silent.

"I expect you're wondering why we're both here?" Mark asked.

Jed nodded. He couldn't recall a joint deputation from both his chief financial officer and sales director before.

"Raj just met with Whitesmith Insurance," Mark said.

Jed drummed his fingers. A meeting between his sales director and their biggest client was nothing remarkable. "And?" he said.

Sweat glistened on Raj's upper lip. "They don't like our Indian call centre," he said. "They want to end our contract."

Jed had been expecting, indeed even hoping for, a technical question. There was nothing he loved more than solving a difficult IT problem. "They can't do that," he snapped. "Since I set up GardNet, I've insisted on huge penalty clauses for all our customers if they terminate early. Whitesmith will have to pay us millions. Billions if I have anything to do with it. I'll see them in court."

"They can do it, and they'd win a legal case, because their contract only has a one month break clause," Mark said. "They were one of our first clients. Our bargaining power was weak. For Whitesmith, we had to agree to terms and conditions we wouldn't accept today."

"We do stand a chance of retaining them as a client," Raj interrupted. "I persuaded them to give us two months to set up a call centre for them in the UK."

"That's impossible," Jed said flatly. "Are you complete idiots? We can't recruit and train an IT helpdesk in the UK in two months, especially with the Christmas holiday period about to start."

"Raj has got a good deal for us in the circumstances," Mark said. "Jed, this contract is worth £20m a year in profits. This way, we get to keep it. It would be a very sorry Christmas indeed if we had to tell our shareholders we'd flushed all that down the toilet. No bonus, and very probably the boot for both of us."

Jed nodded, wincing. They both owned shares in the company – they had set it up, after all – but they'd sold a controlling interest to private equity investors in order to fund expansion. The majority shareholders had been hands off, so far. Why change a winning team? Losers were a different matter.

"I don't know what Whitesmith are so upset about, though," Jed said. "We don't hold their data in India; we have servers right here in London, in Docklands, for that. Our banking clients insisted on it. The Indian guys are just there to answer the dumb IT questions that our clients can't seem to resist asking. Like how do you switch the PC on?"

Raj and Mark exchanged knowing glances.

"It really does get as basic as that," Jed protested. "I fielded those questions every hour in the bad old days when I manned the IT helpline in Birmingham. You know what? I could have been sitting on the end of a phone in another galaxy, and it wouldn't have made a difference."

"It's not simply a matter of data management," Raj said. "Whitesmith staff don't have any confidence in our Indian colleagues. They don't like their accents, they feel it takes too long to receive advice, and half the time it's wrong."

"That's shocking if it's true," Jed said. "I want that call centre manager over here on the next plane."

Raj looked uncomfortable. "I'm not convinced it's an accurate description of our service, by any means," he admitted. "But the customer is king. I'm merely telling you what Whitesmith is saying to me. As it happens, Whitesmith's chairman has political ambitions. I think that's the real driver behind this. They're keen to demonstrate to their customers that they're buying British, so they want a call centre in the UK."

"They've also given you a very specific shopping list of the service levels they want," Mark said.

"Yes. 100% of phone calls must be answered within 30 seconds, with 95% of queries resolved within five minutes."

"That'll cost a fortune," Jed complained.

"Actually, they're receptive to paying more," Raj said. "I believe they'd cover the extra costs. But that's not all. They want Geordie accents. Apparently, they're perceived as the most trustworthy."

"If anyone understands them," Mark murmured.

"I might as well write my resignation letter now," Jed ranted. "We can't simply recruit extra people at the datacentre in Docklands, or even try to find the guys we let go in Birmingham five years ago when we offshored the call handling to India. We have to recruit people in Newcastle, who may know nothing about IT, and we have two months maximum to hire and train them."

"There's another solution," Mark said. "Madrigal has a call centre in South Shields, and it wants to sell it."

"South Shields? Where's that?"

"It's a town near Newcastle," Mark said. "The local accent is almost the same, close enough for Whitesmith to find it acceptable. The staff are highly trained and award winning. And their wages are much lower than they would be in London. Frankly, it's an unemployment blackspot and you can pay people what you like."

"Why is Madrigal selling?"

"Madrigal's exiting the IT support business, except for first line technical support for their own hardware and software. I suspect they can't make money out of the call centre now the focus of that market has moved offshore to India. Ironic, as Whitesmith want us to onshore again."

"OK," Jed said. "Let's talk to Madrigal. Raj – you'll lead the negotiations."

Mark caught Jed's eye. "Please," Jed said.

"The negotiations are commercially sensitive and we should keep them secret," Mark said. "We need a project name."

"Project Shield," Jed suggested.

"One last point," Mark said. "Failure is not an option. We have to buy the call centre from Madrigal. I don't know how much it will cost: £30m? £40m? As your CFO, I could be considered derelict in my duties if we didn't structure this deal tax-efficiently. I think we need to recruit a whizzkid tax planner, and I've found one. He's my squash partner, actually: Boris Brooks. Do you want to meet him before he starts next week?"

"No," Jed said. "Meeting another beancounter is the last thing I need. It's your job, and his, to ensure we pay as little tax as possible. I don't care how you do it. Am I clear?"

"I don't blame you, Jed," Raj said. "We've got too many finance managers already. With all the reports they want, there's barely time to run the business."

"Thanks for your support," Mark fired back.

Jed had almost lost patience. They might be joking with each other, he supposed. It was too exhausting to analyse their behaviour to determine if that was the case. "Stop your bickering, and concentrate on the Madrigal deal," he warned them.

Chapter 3 Andrew's deal

The last of the autumn leaves had finally fallen, forming a golden carpet around St Paul's Church. Andrew Aycliffe hurried back from his lunch appointment in central Birmingham, suspecting from the quickening wind and leaden sky that snow was on its way.

Ruby was waiting in his office, already sitting at his meeting table.

"Make yourself at home," he told her cheerfully, hanging up his coat and scarf. "Would you like a coffee?"

"I've brought some," she replied, gesturing to two cups on the table.

"Ah, thou good and faithful servant," Andrew said, sitting opposite her. "Give me the latest on the call centre, then."

"It's looking promising," Ruby said. "I sent briefing packs yesterday to five targets, all of them likely prospects to buy the division. I've had two expressions of interest so far, both in the £23m to £27m range."

"It's worth more than that," Andrew said. "OK, the call centre isn't part of our core business, and I'd like to sell it so I can return cash to Madrigal's shareholders - but I'm not giving it away."

"Understood," Ruby said.

"I knew you would," Andrew said. He was pleased at the way Ruby was developing as a negotiator. Unlike most sales managers, she was interested in profitability as well as sales targets. "If we can't raise £30m for the South Shields division, we're better off keeping it," he explained.

"I think more bidders will emerge," Ruby said. "That could be one right now." Her smartphone, set to silent mode and placed next to her coffee, was starting to vibrate.

"Why don't you take it?" Andrew suggested. He waited as she spoke to the caller, sensing from her ready smile and animated voice that it was good news. "Well?" he demanded as soon as the call had ended.

"That was Raj Patel," Ruby said. "He was talking high twenties. I bet he'd go above £30m." She blushed. "He's a pleasant fellow to do business with, too. Very personable."

Andrew grinned. "Are you telling me you fancy him?" he teased her.

"No." Ruby laughed. "Never mix business with pleasure."

"Would you make me an offer otherwise?" he said, tongue in cheek.

"Sorry, beards don't do it for me."

Andrew fingered the offending hair on his chin. "Too bad," he said, amused. An awkward thought was beginning to nag him. He stopped smiling. "Ruby, doesn't Raj Patel work for GardNet?"

"That's right," Ruby said.

"Don't speak to him. I won't sell to that bunch."

"Why not?"

"Why not, indeed?" Andrew decided to explain. "It's personal, Ruby. Jed Gardner nearly destroyed my career before it began."

"But," Ruby objected, "Raj is the highest bidder so far."

Andrew would not relent. "By all means include him in your negotiations, but only to push the price up so someone else pays more. I'm not selling the call centre to Jed Gardner's company. End of story."

Chapter 4 Boris catches up

"Another one bites the dust, huh?" Mark grinned. "And you're doing the deed on Valentine's Day too. Corny as the Jolly Green Giant."

"I thought I should make an honest woman of her," Boris told his new boss. "I can't remember if I mentioned the wedding and stag weekend at the interview."

"You didn't." Mark's smile disappeared, and his voice became harsh. "You kept it quiet at the squash club too. I'd heard rumours that she'd suckered you into it, I just didn't realise it would be so soon. That gives me a headache. It took me months to get a budget from our shareholders to recruit a tax manager. Project Shield gave me a reason to do it at last, but I need you to work on tax planning for the project, like, yesterday."

Boris hadn't anticipated difficulties taking holiday. "Do you want to come along to the stag do?" he offered. "It's in Amsterdam, and I'm sure you said you'd be there on business anyway that Friday."

Mark's face settled into its usual amicable expression. "That's the least you can do for me, mate. OK, I think we can accommodate a Friday afternoon off for your stag, as long as you keep your honeymoon short. You're right: Raj Patel and I are seeing a prospective client in Amsterdam on the Friday morning. Raj has to fly straight back, but I'll stay on and hang out with you." He laughed. "The fleshpots of Amsterdam hold a lot more appeal than my usual routine of baby sick and nagging from the wife."

"You're really selling the concept of marriage to me," Boris said wryly. "Melissa's thinking of baby names already. I've felt the pressure ever since she turned thirty."

"You can't back out now, mate, can you? Best you just let Uncle Mark help you get stoned, laid and pissed, not necessarily in that order."

Boris was happy to acquiesce. "Sure, I'll email you all the details – where we're staying, who's going, and so on."

"Anyone I know?"

"A few old schoolfriends. You might have met Lee? Several of the guys at the squash club sponsored him for a charity boxing match last month."

"Yes, rather him than me. I was one of the sponsors," Mark said. "I'm surprised he's paying for a weekend in Amsterdam. Are you staying in a youth hostel, or what? He's a bit of a tightwad. I had to buy his drinks when he popped round to the club to say thanks."

"We're staying at the Grand Hotel Krasnapolsky," Boris said, feeling mildly insulted. He resented the implication that he and his friends were mean. It was true, of course that Lee was short of cash; he had a large family, a mistake Boris didn't intend to copy. The other stags had pooled resources to subsidise Lee's trip.

"I'll book a room there," Mark said. "Sorted."

"Glad you can join us," Boris said. He really should have extended the stag invitation to his squash buddies. A raucous weekend in Amsterdam was some compensation for the white wedding and trimmings that would follow. He felt bold enough now to broach the subject of his honeymoon again. "I'll need time off after the wedding as well. Melissa's booked two weeks in Bali. It's all paid for."

"Jed will want you here, mate, sorry. I guess GardNet can stump up for you to have a holiday once the call centre acquisition is done, all expenses paid."

Boris had known Jed Gardner, briefly, at university. Jed had counted his pennies then, and Boris doubted he would permit his staff a lavish expense account. Rather than say so outright, Boris decided to change tack. "I'd have to pay tax on that. It would be a benefit in kind."

Mark was looking strained. "Ask Jed Gardner for a special dispensation to take your honeymoon in February, then, but don't expect him to be impressed."

"That's another issue we need to discuss. The accounts staff tell me that the company bought a swanky London flat for Jed Gardner. And they say they've settled invoices for helicopter flights to visit his mother. Surely those are taxable benefits for him? I mean, his tax liability will be massive. Do you think he knows?"

"Better ask him. You knew him at uni; you can judge better than me how he'll react." Mark appeared uninterested; surprisingly, given that Boris had only worked for GardNet for two days and had discovered a tax problem already.

Although Jed was CEO of a huge IT company, it was unexpectedly straightforward to secure a meeting with him. Valerie, his PA, said Jed had nothing booked in his diary that day at all, and Boris could see him in ten minutes if he wanted.

Jed was on the phone when Valerie ushered Boris into his luxurious office. "I told you, I've seen enough beancounters," the CEO was saying. He gestured to Boris to sit at a large glass meeting table. The seats, cream leather swivel chairs with s-shaped backs, looked ergonomically designed. Boris found his was easily the most uncomfortable he had ever experienced.

Jed raised an eyebrow and slammed the phone down. "Jonathan Brooks. What the hell are you doing here?" he demanded.

"I'm your new tax manager," Boris replied.

"Yes, so Val says. But I thought I'd seen the last of you when I moved out of that chaotic student flat in Aston."

Boris bridled. "It was clean and tidy enough." It had been a great place to live: sociable, near a good pub, sufficiently organised that he could lay his hands on computers, books and booze when required. Trust Gardner to have different memories, with his OCD tendencies. Of course, there had been the disagreement over Melissa too.

Jed didn't waste any time in mentioning it. "You were seeing that sensational flute player, Melissa."

Boris couldn't resist boasting. "We're getting married in February," he said.

Jed's eyes narrowed. "I see. That was what you came here to tell me?"

"No. I'm concerned from a corporate governance perspective. I understand you're living in a company flat, and GardNet has been paying for private helicopter flights. There may be a large income tax liability for you. I expect the GardNet board considered all that when agreeing to the expenditure, but I thought I should…"

"What is this bullshit?" Jed rose to his feet. "Our meeting is over. You're our tax manager. I'm paying you to make sure I don't have to pay any tax on my flat, or anything else. Got it?"

Nonplussed, Boris muttered, "Sure."

"Good. Tell that idiot, Mark Trelawney, that I want to see him now. He told me you were going to save us millions, not go to frigging HMRC and tell them to help themselves from my bank account."

"I will be saving you millions on Project Shield," Boris said, "and I'm sure I can keep your tax on the flat as low as possible."

"Glad to hear it. I was beginning to regret allowing Trelawney to recruit a tax manager." Jed had stopped shouting, although he still had that sulky look that Boris remembered from their student days. "Why on earth would Mark call you Boris, by the way?"

"Everyone does. I do myself. It started as a joke and just seemed to stick. I'm a dead ringer for Boris Johnson, apparently."

"Half the size, though."

Boris felt his cheeks redden. "He's only six inches taller," he argued.

"Still." Jed walked to his office door, opened it and started talking to Valerie. He didn't so much as turn his head when Boris said goodbye.

Mentioning his honeymoon to Jed at this point would be career suicide. Boris returned to the finance department, wishing he had poisoned Jed's coffee when they were flatmates. It would have saved him grief now.

"What did he say?" Mark wanted to know.

"He was less than amused at the thought of paying tax. Why didn't you warn me he would throw all his toys out of the pram?"

"You're a big boy, Boris," Mark said, rather spoiling the phrase by adding, "in a manner of speaking." He put a hand on Boris's shoulder. "It's up to you to manage your relationship with Jed; adapt your working style to suit him. We all have to do it. Anyway, I thought you'd shared a flat with him at university."

"I did, but he was very quiet then. Morose, rather than argumentative. He liked Melissa." Boris shook his head. "He never stood a chance with her. Melissa knows what a real man looks like. I imagined Jed would be over all that, but I found out differently when I said I was engaged to her."

"What? Jed Gardner fancies a woman?" Mark whistled. "I always thought he was completely asexual. I've never seen him interested in either men or women."

"He likes the way she plays the flute."

"You've said enough," Mark leered.

Chapter 5 Jed's night out

Jed's meeting with Boris had unnerved him. Only music would lower his stress levels, clarify the confusion swirling within him. He sank into his chair and scrolled through the music files on his laptop. Debussy would soothe him, though it also transported him back to Aston University, and the day he met Melissa.

He had already begun to dislike his flatmates, and in particular, their messiness: the coffee cups waiting to be washed, the dishes stacked higgledy-piggledy in the cupboard, the stray hairs and soap scum in the bath tub. Gathering his courage, he resolved to tackle Jonathan, who was studying law. He at least ought to be receptive to a set of house rules.

"You know, Jon," he said, "You guys make too much mess in the kitchen. It looks like a nuclear bomb hit it." He was proud that he had remembered to use humour to defuse a difficult conversation, a technique that Eleanor had taught him. He also rather liked the phrase. He had overheard it only yesterday, and mentally filed it away for a rainy day.

If he had hoped for appreciation, he was sadly disappointed. Jonathan hardly looked at him. "Not now, Jed. I'm on my way to grab some culture. A concert. Lee-ay-prez middy dee un fawn."

"L'après-midi d'un faune?" Eleanor's favourite piece. Jed was stunned. From the pounding bass-laden dirges emerging from Jonathan's room, he had thought his flatmate was into heavy metal.

"Yes," Jonathan said impatiently. "Want to come along? We've got ten minutes to run there."

The concert was in an old chapel near their campus. It was free for student cardholders. They arrived two minutes before it started, and had to sit at the back. Jed watched, hardly less astonished than before, as Jonathan gawped open-mouthed at the chamber orchestra. Once the music began, Jed closed his eyes and surrendered to the feeling of tranquillity. He could truly imagine a summer's day in Somerset. The flautist was particularly fine, he thought. He must congratulate her.

"Look at that! Melissa Melons." The piece was over, and Jonathan was digging him in the ribs and pointing at the flautist, a blonde girl wearing a low-cut black ball gown.

"She does play well," Jed said.

"What?"

"I mean, she has real talent. We should talk to her."

"Too right," Jonathan said.

It was hardly surprising that Melissa was mobbed by young men after the concert. Jonathan proved rather successful at elbowing his way past the crush, Jed trailing in his wake.

Jed hardly had time to say, rather stiffly and formally, that he felt her technique was superb. He was interrupted by Jonathan, who launched into a lengthy apology for not bringing her flowers. He felt the performance merited a large bouquet, and perhaps he could take her to dinner the following evening instead?

"I've got a date," Jonathan said smugly as they left the hall. "Fancy a beer?"

"I'm a Quaker." He was still keeping the faith then, Eleanor's faith, so drink was out of the question. He'd returned to the flat alone.

Still alone, albeit now in his spacious and ordered office, Jed sighed. The music had stopped and the sky outside was darkening, London's tall cityscape brightened by neon advertising and the fluorescent squares of distant windows. Regrets had barely troubled him before, but he wished now that he could have spoken and acted differently at that moment in the chapel. He suspected he would be just as gauche if confronted with a similar situation again. It was men like Jonathan, or Boris as he appeared to call himself now, who knew how to turn on the charm.

His phone rang. "Jed?" It was Valerie. "You'll recall, I'm leaving early today and I won't be back until the New Year. Would you like me to book a helicopter to take you to Somerset for Christmas?"

"Yes." He added, as Eleanor had taught him, "Please," and then, as if a faraway bell chimed in his memory banks, said, "Merry Christmas, Val."

Chapter 6 Jed's Christmas

GardNet's Christmas party was billed as a night to remember: dinner in a swish London hotel, followed by dancing to tribute bands. Jed would have preferred to forget all about it, but he knew that convention demanded both a lavish celebration and the CEO's attendance. He began the evening by standing with Mark at the entrance to the function room, gravely wishing his employees a Merry Christmas and thanking them for their work during the year. Hovering waiters plied the partygoers with champagne, which was off limits to Jed. Although no longer a practising Quaker, he did not touch alcohol. He would rather be bored rigid than lose control of himself to a bunch of chemicals.

"I'm very grateful for the difference you've made to GardNet," he began to say to Boris Brooks, then realised the man had worked at GardNet for barely a week.

"Thank you. You've met my fiancée, Melissa, before of course," Boris said.

Without a flicker of recognition, Melissa shook Jed's hand. She looked exactly the same as on that night in Aston: blonde, pale and fine-featured with the most amazingly long, elegant fingers.

"Do you still play the flute? I saw you give an incredible performance of l'après-midi d'un faune at an old chapel in Birmingham many years ago."

Melissa glowed. "I was studying at the Conservatoire there. Yes, I do still perform, as a matter of fact." She reached into a handbag, bright pink like her dress. "Here's a flyer for my next concert, in the New Year. I'd be delighted to see you there."

"The Orchestra of London," he intoned, carefully folding the leaflet and putting it in his breast pocket. "I would be equally delighted."

"We mustn't stop you enjoying some champagne," Mark said, taking two fizzing glasses from a proffered tray and handing them to the engaged couple. He whispered to Jed, "We'll have to speed up the glad handing. There's a queue building."

That was music to Jed's ears, and he barked his thanks and greetings abruptly to the rest of the partygoers.

"I thought we could have a small table together," Mark said. "Helena's here of course, and our other companions are the HR bunny and someone she's brought with her. And before you ask, the someone is female and is not the HR bunny's partner. I have it on very good authority that our bunny is a confirmed heterosexual."

Helena was Mark's wife, a banker who had arranged a lot of GardNet's funding in the early days. Jed was as comfortable in her presence as he could be in anyone's. Lucy, the chirpy young woman whom he and Mark had christened the HR bunny, was another matter entirely. He had no time for her fluffy policies about treating his team with respect. As far as he was concerned, his only obligation was to pay them handsomely and theirs in turn was to do as they were told. Her friend, however, was surprisingly good company.

"Jeannie," she introduced herself as he sat next to her. "I'm a friend of Lucy's and a bit of a party animal. And you are Jed Gardner, the computer genius, I understand?"

With Helena on his left and Jeannie on his right, the conversation flowed better than Jed had expected. Jeannie did not know a great deal about security algorithms, but she seemed to love hearing about them.

"What do you do?" he asked her, after spending thirty minutes discussing his latest plan for improving GardNet's firewall.

"I'm a dating coach," she said. "Would you like my card?"

"I don't suppose I'll need it," Jed said. At that moment, he glimpsed a flash of bright pink at the next table, where Melissa was chatting vivaciously with Boris Brooks. A pang of jealousy enveloped him. He scanned Jeannie's card into his smartphone.

"I would really like to explore with you some funding options for Project Shield," Helena told him.

"We could go back to my office and do that now if you like," said Jed, seizing on it as an escape route from the party. Melissa's presence had made the function even more of a torture than usual. He could not help both glancing at her and feeling irritated that she was absorbed with Brooks. They were cuddling each other on the dance floor. A band, allegedly lookalikes for the Fab Four, had begun to play Beatles covers.

"It can wait until the New Year," Mark said, reaching out to hold his wife's hand. "We should be dancing, I think."

"You can dance with me, Jed," Lucy, the HR bunny, offered.

Mark elbowed him in the ribs. "Just for one number," he hissed. "That's all you have to do. Show willing, eh?"

Jed allowed Lucy to lead him to the parquet oval in the centre of the room, ignoring the clapping and cheering that he suspected Mark had initiated among their employees. He swayed awkwardly in time to the music, Lucy bobbing in front of him.

"Thank you, I really must leave now and do some work," he told her.

Mark took him to one side. "You could have been in there, mate," he suggested.

Jed waved him away impatiently. The remark wasn't worthy of a reply.

The next morning, a car collected him from his flat at St Pancras and delivered him to the London Heliport at Battersea. He occasionally travelled from Luton Airport, taking advantage of a first-class ticket on one of the intercity trains passing through both stations, but they would be too crowded at this time of year.

Helicopter trips to see Eleanor were one of Jed's few luxuries. He always used the same pilot. Geoff was in his fifties and allegedly had a wealth of stories about flying the rich and famous around Europe. Jed had never heard any of them. He had made it clear from the start that he preferred peace and quiet. Geoff honoured his wishes, making sure Jed was well-supplied with coffee and then busying himself with the flight.

Despite excellent noise-cancelling headphones, the clatter of the blades still resounded in his ears. The flight was quick, however. Jed had brought a technical magazine to read, and barely had time to flick through it and drink his coffee before they landed near Bath. As usual, Geoff had arranged to land in the grounds of Cherry Trees, and he helped Jed take his bags to the reception area before wishing him a cheery farewell.

Coloured lights festooned the windows of the house, a gracious old Bath stone mansion. There was a lavishly decorated Christmas tree in the television room, to which he was ushered by a nurse upon his arrival.

"Here she is," the nurse said. "Look, Ellie, it's your son, Gerald."

"She's called Eleanor," Jed said.

Eleanor wore the sort of sensible clothes she had always favoured: a brown wool jumper and tweed slacks. She was sitting in a wing armchair with a wipe-clean vinyl surface. At Jed's approach, her eyes swivelled round to meet his. She had been watching television, and he noted approvingly that it was a classical concert. She must have been enjoying it.

"Hello, Eleanor. I've brought you chocolates," he said. Rose and violet creams. Val had popped out for them, after he had stressed to her that these were the sort that Eleanor always liked; they, and no other, would do.

The old lady was silent. She did not seem to know who he was. He was used to that. Eventually, she grabbed the box out of his hand. "Thank you," she said.

He was pleased to hear her voice again. "Let me open it and we can share them," he said. "I've got marvellous news. I think I've found the girl I want to marry."

"About time," Eleanor said. Perhaps she did recognise him. She pushed aside a straggle of grey hair that had escaped from her neat bun and made its way in front of her left eye.

That was the extent of the conversation he was going to extract from her. Eleanor had seldom been one for small talk anyway, which suited Jed. She never asked him if he continued to attend Quaker meetings. He did not, as it happened, although as they too were largely silent, he had quite enjoyed them. She munched on the chocolates with pleasure as he told her about Melissa and her exceptional musical talent.

"Why don't we save the rest for later?" The nurse had noticed the first layer of chocolates was empty.

Jed murmured his assent. "Well, I must be going now," he said to Eleanor. "I'll see you tomorrow, on Christmas Day."

"We should ask your new friend, Melissa, to tea," Eleanor said, with a happy smile. "You can both play with your train set."

That brought a tear to his eye. He wondered if his old train set was still laid out in the attic of her cottage, as it had been when he was a boy. What a pleasant adventure it had been, to bring a ladder to the loft hatch and then play on the bare boards of that huge, empty, quiet space, completely alone. He really should ask Val to make sure someone kept an eye on the cottage in Somerset. The property had lain unoccupied for two years, ever since Eleanor's mind began to fail and he had reluctantly arranged for her to move to Cherry Trees.

As a Quaker, Christmas should mean nothing to Eleanor. The rest of the community at Cherry Trees would be celebrating it, though, and Jed did not want Eleanor to feel excluded. "I would like to leave a card and Christmas present in her room," he told the nurse before he left. He had wrapped a new CD featuring Sir Simon Rattle, a conductor he knew Eleanor favoured.

The nurse acquiesced, although she said, "We tend to let the residents open them at breakfast."

Eleanor's room was upstairs, with a view of lawns and clipped box hedges in the extensive grounds. It smelled of roses and was neat and clean. Photographs of Jed as a boy, either alone or scowling next to his cousins, were on display. There were several Christmas cards on the windowsill, a vase of pink carnations on her dressing table.

Having satisfied himself that Eleanor was still happy and well-supported, as she should be for the large fee he was paying Cherry Trees, Jed left. A car had been booked to take him and his luggage to the nearby country house hotel where he was staying. He ordered coffee and sandwiches, took out his laptop and became totally absorbed in his work once more.

On Christmas Day, a local children's choir had been booked to sing carols at Cherry Trees in the morning. There would then be a special meal for the residents, with turkey and trimmings. The carers respected Eleanor's vegetarian diet and assured Jed there would be a nut roast for her.

He arrived just as the carols were finishing and was surprised to see most of Eleanor's surviving relatives there: her younger sister, Virginia and elderly husband, and their two children. Darren and Monica were both about the same age as him, and as children they had played together, or at least in the same room. The Gardner genes, squat, dark and beak-nosed, were very much in evidence. Perhaps the nurses were comparing the rest of the family with Jed's tall, thin, sandy appearance.

Virginia broke the ice. "Merry Christmas, Jed. That was a lovely present you gave Eleanor, wasn't it?"

Thus prompted, Eleanor thanked him, and they all wished each other a Merry Christmas.

"I expect there will be crackers for you, Eleanor, and mince pies," Virginia said. "It would be nice to join you, but I already have a turkey in the oven back at the house in Bath. You're welcome to come back with us, Jed, you know. We can always squeeze an extra place out of the table."

"Sorry, I have work to do."

"On Christmas Day, dear?"

Even so, she did not press him further. Jed knew that Virginia, a Quaker herself, only observed Christmas traditions for the sake of her family. His cousins and their father did not share her faith.

The bank holiday would have been very different if Eleanor had remained of sound mind. Jed missed listening to music with her, and her gentle, kind wisdom. She had always been able to explain the world to him in a way that others could not, helping him to make sense of his surroundings.

He returned to his hotel and ordered sandwiches again. Instead of powering up his laptop, he strolled in the wooded parkland around the buildings. It was a cold, dry day and he enjoyed drinking in the clean air. A railway line ran along one edge of the grounds. No trains would be running on Christmas Day, yet he leaned on the ivy-clad wall that formed the boundary, looking across it to the steep drop and track below. Like scenes from a film, he let his mind flit between memories from his childhood.

His first reminiscence might well have been false. Eleanor had told him the story so many times, it was as if he recalled it himself. On her first visit to the orphanage, she was refused access to the babies. "Those cute little things were reserved for bright, shiny couples," she said. "I didn't mind. I didn't want a baby anyway, with all the crying, mess and training. So Matron took me to see the three and four-year-olds."

The small children were happily sharing toys in the home's spacious playroom, shrieking and laughing. "Apart from one," Eleanor said. "You were sitting in a corner, hugging yourself, a blank expression on your face. 'You won't want Gerald,' Matron told me. 'He's never said a word.'"

Nobody dictated to Eleanor. Perhaps Matron had realised that, and saw her as a convenient way of disposing of a troublesome child. More likely, Matron had not intended to set Eleanor a challenge at all, but luckily for Jed, the peace campaigner had risen to it. She strolled over to the little boy and set three red wooden bricks in front of him.

"How many bricks, Gerald?" she asked quietly.

"Three," he whispered.

It was the first time he had smiled, Matron said. She could not wait to send him away with Eleanor then, although Eleanor had to foster him at first. It was difficult for unmarried women to adopt in those days, and she had to pull strings to make the law recognise him as her son two years later.

That was not all Eleanor had done. She built her whole life around Jed, at first working part-time as a district nurse so she could school him at home. There had been a rocky first week at primary school, when he spoke to no one, and that was enough for her to reject the state system and take on his education herself. Later, when she felt he needed more advanced teaching, she found a job as matron at an independently run Quaker secondary school. Together, they would cycle there each day through five miles of country lanes, occasionally using Eleanor's old Land Rover in the poorest weather.

Virginia had been a constant in his childhood, too, always looking after him when Eleanor could not. Perhaps he should have accepted her offer of Christmas lunch, but what would he have said to her? He was always lost for words, while Virginia's family liked to chat at the dinner table. It was better to leave them to it. He was only being considerate, he told himself, and Eleanor would approve of that.

Before the last of the Christmas daylight faded, Jed walked back towards the hotel buildings. There was a duck pond on the way. He shared the remains of his sandwiches with the birds.

Chapter 7 Taylor's foreign foray

Taylor knew her friend could be bossy, but hadn't expected Annie-Belle to reveal it as soon as they arrived at JFK for the eight hour flight to Amsterdam. A tall blonde whirlwind, Annie-Belle marched straight to the first class check-in desk. To Taylor's relief, the area was devoid of queues and therefore possibilities for embarrassment.

"You should be giving us both an upgrade," Annie-Belle demanded. "My friend is a travel journalist. She's writing a piece about Airlite luggage."

Taylor felt herself blushing. Her face was probably as red as her hair. Airlite's marketing manager, Martin Parsons, had admitted to her that his brand was hardly Louis Vuitton.

The check-in clerk's demeanour suggested she'd heard it all before. "Let me see your tickets."

Taylor handed over the emails confirming their booking.

"I see you've checked in online already. Well," the clerk's smile was blazing, and her gaze hard, "there's nothing more I can do, I'm afraid. Your seats are confirmed. Have a great flight, ladies."

They were in the central section of economy class, near a couple of families with small children. "I see enough children at work," Annie-Belle grumbled.

"Never mind. You can have plenty of the free booze, and you won't notice them anymore. How about we call the hostess over to have some champagne?"

She'd forgotten that her friend had forsworn alcohol. Annie-Belle wasted no time in reminding her.

"I'll drink your share," Taylor promised, signalling to the hostess. "At least on a plane, no one asks for ID." While she was well over twenty-one, she was constantly being told she didn't look it.

The hotel was another thorn of contention.

"Airlite can't possibly expect you to stay in a place like this," Annie-Belle said.

"Martin Parsons told me it was a very convenient hotel, right by the central station in Amsterdam," Taylor pointed out. "That's why he booked us in here."

"Convenient for what? This is the red light district," Annie-Belle sniffed. "And there are funny smells emerging from that coffee shop next door. Don't imagine I don't know what they are."

Taylor admitted defeat. Annie-Belle was right. Martin's choice was a dilapidated fleapit, and in this area, was likely rented by the hour. "Let's find us a coffee shop." She noticed Annie-Belle's horrified face. "No, not that one. Let's just walk on down the road. I'll make some phone calls and find a better hotel."

She had no intention of paying for it. The flights, which Martin had assured her would be reimbursed just as soon as he saw her travel piece, had maxed out her credit card. She had, however, arranged to see some Dutch fashion designers and write a separate feature about them. It was time to call in some favours.

"I can get you in the New Yorker," she trilled on her phone. It had the desired effect. One of the designers had done a show at the Krasnapolsky, 'the best hotel in town,' he told Taylor. They gave him mate's rates and he would pay for a room there.

Annie-Belle, sipping a cappuccino, looked askance. "How will you get a story about him into the New Yorker?" she asked.

Taylor shrugged. "I didn't make any promises. Anyhow, they might take an article about him. I interned at the paper one summer. I have contacts."

The Krasnapolsky was everything they both wanted: an upscale hotel, bright and warm to combat the chill of a Dutch winter. Annie-Belle looked longingly at the twin beds in their large room. Sleep hadn't come easily on the crowded plane.

"I'll fix us a coffee," Taylor said. "I'm told the best way to overcome jet lag is to stay awake as long as possible."

"You were told? Haven't you been to Europe before?" Annie-Belle asked.

"This is my first travel article. I usually write about style and beauty."

"Maybe that's why Airlite thought you'd settle for that dump on the Warmoestraat," Annie-Belle said. "Cheapskates. A large company like that could afford something better. And club class air tickets."

"Martin Parsons said his budget had been cut. Anyway, I thought it was a great deal: an expenses-paid trip to Europe and a chance to raise my profile." She yawned. "Let's grab some more caffeine, or I'll never get through the day. I've lined up two meetings with clothing designers later. Like to come along?"

Annie-Belle did not. She wanted to stay in the heated room. Taylor shivered, preparing once more to negotiate the bracingly cold wind blowing through the cobbled streets. With the concierge's help, she had a tram map and a rough idea of the route to her first appointment.

Chapter 8 Boris seeks R&R

It was past seven o'clock on Friday evening by the time Boris arrived at the cocktail bar.

"You're late," Mark pointed out.

"Air traffic control problems. I switched to the Eurostar. How was your business meeting?"

"All the better for having finished. You know how it is; in most companies, the CEO would be schmoozing important customers, but we can't let Jed loose on them."

"How on earth did he end up as CEO?"

Mark shrugged. "He set the company up, mate. And he's a genius. I'd ease him out if I could, but our shareholders won't hear of it. Anyway, enough of that. I'm here to party." Mark looked around appreciatively. "I like the Krasnapolsky. A good choice, Boris. Great bar, and not far from the action. When are the rest of your stags turning up?"

"Tomorrow morning. Their flights were delayed too."

"Then we're in luck. Two's the perfect number. Take a peek at Miss Gorgeous and Blondie over there."

Sitting together, just two tables away from them, were a tall blonde and a girl with long, wavy red hair. Mark was clearly attracted to the redhead, who was petite and pretty, her short red dress revealing a shapely figure and slim legs.

"You're a married man," Boris said. "Leave this to me. I can handle the both of them."

Mark ignored him, hailing the waiter. "Give the ladies another drink, with my compliments," he said. "And I'd like a bottle of champagne and four glasses over here." He nudged Boris. "GardNet's paying for the drinks out of our travel budget, OK? If we play our cards right, we won't need to visit the red light district tonight. Anyway, it's more fun for free."

Boris couldn't bear to say there would be no tax relief for GardNet on the drinks. When they were back in the office, he must talk to Mark about improving the company's control over its costs. For now, he might as well enjoy his boss' lavish expense account.

The inevitable happened. Miss Gorgeous came over to thank them.

"It was a pleasure," Mark said. "Why don't you and your friend join us for the evening? Boris and I are stuck here on our own and we need some help drinking this." He gestured to the champagne.

"I'd love to, but Annie-Belle doesn't drink."

"Let's see if we can persuade her," said Boris, flashing what he hoped was a roguish grin. "I'm Boris, by the way. And you are?"

"Taylor."

Only a Yank, or the unfortunate child of a celebrity, would have a name like that. "I can tell you're American," Boris said. "From New York?"

"Ambertown, New Jersey."

"You must tell us all about it," said Mark, slipping into the conversation smoothly to Boris' silent irritation. "Take a seat."

That worked. Once Taylor was sitting with them, Annie-Belle had to follow suit.

"What brings you girls to Amsterdam?" Boris asked.

"I'm a travel writer," Taylor said.

"She's never been out of the USA before. This is her first commissioned piece," Annie-Belle interjected.

"Oh?" Mark sounded surprised.

"Yes," Annie-Belle said. "Taylor's been asked to road test Airlite luggage, and write an article about it."

"That should be air test, surely?" Boris said.

Nobody laughed.

Mark raised an eyebrow. "Isn't Airlite the suitcase of choice for drug smugglers?"

"How do you know?" Boris asked. That evinced at least a snort from Annie-Belle.

"I've read that the case has a hollow shell, and it's easy to fill it with drugs and reseal it," Mark said. "Be careful what kind of road testing you give that luggage."

"I have no intention of buying drugs," Taylor said hotly.

Mark looked chagrined. "Joke," he said.

In the momentary silence that followed, Taylor's phone rang.

"Let's order more drinks," Boris said while she was answering it. He knew a little Dutch, and asked the waiter to add vodka to both Taylor's tequila sunrise and Annie-Belle's orange juice, ignoring Mark's perplexed expression. That would give the drinks some oomph, and with any luck, rescue the evening.

"You'll never guess what." Taylor was fuming. "Martin Parsons from Airlite wants us to go back to that dreadful hotel on the Warmoestraat. We can't have an authentic Amsterdam experience otherwise, he says."

"You'll have a better time here with us," Boris said, exchanging glances with Mark.

"It has to be an improvement on my day so far, finding I've been booked into the hotel from hell and then interviewing gay fashion designers."

"No gays here," Mark purred.

"I'm not going back to that hotel," Annie-Belle stated flatly.

"You don't have to. I told him to get lost. I just hope he still pays for my work," Taylor said, furiously knocking back her tequila sunrise.

Boris somehow doubted that Airlite would be paying her. He could make Amsterdam memorable for Taylor, though. Grinning, he imagined giving her a very high quality experience indeed. He waved to the staff for another drink. The contents of her glass had seemingly disappeared in seconds.

The tequila was working. Taylor's wide green eyes fixed on his. "Have I met you somewhere before?" she asked.

"Who, Boris?" Mark said, before Boris had a chance to speak. "You've probably seen him on TV, or in the papers. As Mayor of London, he's become famous worldwide." He maintained a straight face. "Why do you think we're staying at the Krasnapolsky? Nothing but the best for BoJo."

"I knew it!" Taylor said.

Boris choked on his champagne. Mark nudged him. "Got to go to the gents, mate."

Boris followed him.

"Good," Mark said. "I'm glad you had the nous to go with me." He glanced at the two girls, who were now deep in conversation. "Look, Miss Gorgeous fancies you. Or she fancies you as long as she thinks you're Boris Johnson, anyway."

Boris groaned. "But it's a joke, and an old, not particularly good, one at that."

"Play along with it mate. You want to get into her knickers, don't you? It's your only chance."

"What about Blondie?"

Mark sighed. "I'll take care of her. Things I do for you, mate." He added, "Keep the vodkas coming. That's one thing you've got right."

"Whatever your plans for Blondie, hurry up. I want to be alone with big tits Taylor."

Boris' wish was soon granted. Doubtless fatigued by the secret vodkas, Annie-Belle announced she was tired.

"You're staying here, aren't you?" Mark said. "I'll take you back to your room."

"Aren't you coming?" she asked Taylor. "We're sharing, after all."

There was a glint in Mark's eye. "You owe me," he mouthed at Boris.

"Another drink?" Boris offered, hoping Mark would sign his expense claim. To his relief, he recalled that he only needed to give Mark's room number to their waiter. "What's your room like, by the way?"

"Fine. Why do you ask?" Taylor drawled.

"Mine's a suite, with a Jacuzzi. All to myself. Why not come along with me, check it out for your travel article?"

She looked interested. He added, "I can order more drinks if you like, and dinner if you're hungry. It'll be quiet; a bit more relaxing than the bar."

"Great idea," Taylor agreed.

Boris put an arm around her shoulders and guided her to the lift. He had a feeling Taylor would be putty in his hands. He was not wrong. Once in his suite, she embraced him and closed her eyes. It was clear she wanted a kiss, and more. He slipped his tongue between her lips, held her against him and felt her lovely breasts, firm and warm against his chest, her skin separated from his only by their thin clothing.

"I think my Jacuzzi was made for sharing," he murmured, painfully aware that he had sweated on the long journey to Amsterdam. He would have to add copious amounts of bubble bath to the tub to disguise the odour. The last thing he wanted was for Taylor to recoil when he undressed.

"Yes," Taylor breathed. She fished an iPad from her handbag.

"What?" Boris was alarmed.

"You know. Everybody does this now. So we can look at ourselves afterwards." Taylor laughed merrily.

"And start again?" Boris chuckled. "Yes, indeed."

Boris was bleary-eyed when he heard his phone ring the next morning. Its ring tone was insistent, a jolly tune that he had downloaded once in a fit of drunken enthusiasm. He shook off the bed covers and fumbled in his jacket pocket for the phone, noticing that Taylor was still asleep. Hardly surprising that she was dead to the world, after piling a day's work and an athletic night with him on top of her jet lag. He licked his lips, admiring the curve of her breasts and remembering how they had yielded to his touch.

"How did you get on?" Mark wanted to know.

"A class act. Anything I wanted, she was up for it," Boris said, taking care to keep his voice down in case Taylor suddenly awoke. "How about you?"

"No chance with Blondie," said Mark. "Flat chested, tight assed bitch." He mimicked Annie-Belle's high-pitched drawl. "'I have no interest in seeing you naked. I'm saving myself for my wedding night.' I've no reason to disbelieve her."

"Bad luck," Boris said. "Look, I'll catch up with you later. I plan to spend more time with my new friend going through the rest of the Kama Sutra."

"Oh no you don't." Mark sounded alarmed. "The rest of your stags will be here soon, won't they? It's your duty to lead us carousing through Amsterdam. I'm expecting wine, women, song and dope from you, and I wouldn't be leaving my wife for the weekend otherwise. Give Miss Gorgeous the boot, or, if you really can't resist her charms, ask her to leave you alone for a bit. You can promise her brunch tomorrow and tell her you've got business to do right now."

"On a Saturday?"

"You could be a drug smuggler, couldn't you? It sounds like she knows one already, that dodgy Airlite bloke she was talking about. Or, as she thinks you're BoJo, tell her you're opening a supermarket. For God's sake," his voice was strained, "make something up."

Regretfully, Boris switched on the Nespresso machine and began to rehearse his excuses.

Chapter 9 Taylor's breakfast in Amsterdam

Taylor was ecstatic. "He's such a gentleman," she chirped to Annie-Belle.

"Why won't he come sightseeing with us today?" Annie-Belle was sceptical.

"He's delivering training in social skills to a group of businessmen."

"At the weekend?" Annie-Belle shrugged. "We can have fun without him. I want to do a boat trip on the Dutch canals before they freeze over. Then we can go shopping to fill those Airlite suitcases. And I've read this is a very cultural city. Isn't there an art gallery with that Sunflowers picture? You know, Van Gogh?" She pronounced it 'Van Go.'

Taylor acquiesced. Annie-Belle's suggestions would add colour to her travel article. In January, Amsterdam had a bleak beauty, the grey skies, skeletal trees and brown brick buildings reflected in the water on which the city seemed to float. Airlite would expect some reference to sightseeing as well the indestructibility of its suitcases.

The girls were so busy that Taylor had no time to pine for Boris, and was about to crash out, exhausted, on her pristine bed when she noticed he had emailed.

The message was terse: 'Brunch. Tomorrow, 11.30. Café Americain.'

Taylor replied with a heart, and attached several stills of Boris' performance the previous evening. She slipped easily into a deep sleep. Her fatigue was such that Annie-Belle had to shake her awake on Sunday morning.

"It's eleven o'clock."

Taylor fixed her face and hair in minutes, tottering to the tram stop nearby in skyscraper heels. She had already chosen a short, emerald-green dress to flatter her hair and eyes.

A jazz band was in full swing at the art deco Café Americain, and most of the places were full. "Table for one, Madam?"

"I'm meeting someone." Taylor squinted furiously. Boris was nowhere to be seen.

"Do you have a name?"

"Johnson."

"No bookings in that name, Madam. You are welcome to come in and see if your friends are here. If they are not, we can always find a table for you."

Taylor smiled. She was aware that her looks opened doors. She set off for the furthest corner of the room, which was large and actually rather dimly lit on a grey January day.

"Taylor."

Someone was grabbing her arm. She wheeled round, confused. It was Boris' friend. What was his name? Mark.

"You walked straight past us."

"Us?" She suddenly realised Boris was sitting with a group of half a dozen men, most of them taller. "I beg your pardon. I thought this brunch was just you and me, Boris. Two's company, six is a crowd."

"We thought he might need help handling you," Mark smirked. "He was dog-tired yesterday."

Boris had the grace to look embarrassed. "My email about brunch was addressed to a few people," he admitted. "Taylor, did you really mean to hit 'Reply to All'?"

The awareness of what she had done dawned on her, just as she saw they were all leering at her.

"You can put your red lips round mine, any time," Mark said brutally.

"Behave," Boris told him.

"You didn't, did you, Jonathan?" Mark said.

"Jonathan?" Taylor asked.

"That's his name," Mark said.

"Not – Boris Johnson?" She was puzzled.

"It's a long-running gag," Boris said. "No, I'm not Boris Johnson. I'm told I look like him, though." His friends, Mark included, were sniggering.

"You both lied to me?" Taylor bit her lip. Shocked as she was, she had the presence of mind to slap Mark's face. She noticed his eyes lighting up, as if he'd enjoyed it.

Boris flinched.

"Don't worry," Taylor said, her face flushed and her voice high, "I'm not giving second helpings."

"Of anything," Mark said. "I should think not. Our Boris has had his fun. He's getting married on Valentine's Day."

She stormed out. It was only when she pushed open the restaurant door, feeling assailed by the icy air of the cobbled square, that she began to cry.

38

Annie-Belle was surprisingly sympathetic. "I didn't want to mention it before," she admitted, "but I realised there was something weird about them when Mark walked me back to our room on Friday."

"Do tell." Taylor's anger diffused as she surrendered to curiosity.

"He said he thought I liked to be in charge."

"Bossy, you mean?"

Annie-Belle looked askance. "Don't interrupt. You'll never guess what happened next. He took a ping pong bat out of his briefcase."

"And?"

"He said he wanted me to use it. On his naked butt. Of course, I told him to get lost." She flicked her long blonde hair indignantly. "That's not all. After that, he tried to grab my boobs. I socked his jaw."

Taylor's black mood was lifting. She laughed. "I noticed he hadn't shaved. That'll be why. To hide his bruises."

"Taylor, they're a pair of losers. Forget them."

Chapter 10 Jed's love letter

"You're fired," Jed said, slamming the phone down. It immediately rang again. The screen said 'Valerie.'

"What is it?"

"I have Mark Trelawney outside your office."

"Tell him to wait ten minutes. And get me an espresso. Please."

A tension headache was pounding through his temples. Jed took a couple of paracetamol tablets from a jar in his desk drawer, gulping them down without water.

Mark often swaggered, but not today. "I suppose you've fired Raj again?" he said anxiously.

"How do you know?"

"He phoned me first with the news that Madrigal won't play ball. Their call centre is off the market." Mark ran a finger across his throat. "Jed, you can't keep giving Raj the boot whenever he brings you bad news. How many times has it been now?"

"Five. He's screwed up five times. I was crazy to take him back. I won't do it again."

Mark put his head in his hands. "Jed, he's a great sales director. You'll have to rescind the dismissal, and thank your lucky stars he never takes it personally. It's not his fault Madrigal won't sell. Their negotiator simply said Andrew Aycliffe, the CEO, wanted to keep the call centre."

"Why?" Jed asked.

Mark shrugged. "Perhaps Aycliffe just changed his mind."

"I think he wants us to pay more. People always have a reason."

That was what Eleanor had drummed into him. "People always have reasons, Jed. You need to look at their eyes, at the way they move, to see what they really want."

Before she told him that, he was always in trouble at school. One child would dare him to hit another, and he would do it without a second thought. Asked by a teacher if he would like to sit at the front of the classroom, he would answer 'No', little realising it was a command rather than a request.

He had found a book about body language in the school library, and with practice, began to identify the occasions when his classmates were being sly, and when his teachers expected to be obeyed. Those lessons would stand him in good stead now. Not least, he divined that Mark, like him, was at the end of his tether. Jed made a calculated judgement: he must restrain himself from expressing his frustration through anger, and listen to Mark instead.

"We really need to buy that company from Madrigal, don't we?" he asked.

Mark nodded. "Yes. Without it, our biggest client will leave without compensating us. Jobs will go at GardNet, ours included. Your flat would have to be sold."

"OK. Project Shield has to happen. I'm taking personal charge of the negotiations."

Mark's face was a picture of scepticism. "Are you sure? Seriously, we need to keep Raj as well. In fact, I'm not leaving your office until you reinstate him."

"If you insist," Jed sighed. "I'll email Raj now."

"Thanks," Mark said. "And go easy on him, Jed, OK? Some of us don't mind being shouted at occasionally. We can live with a bit of discipline, you might say. Raj isn't like that. It stresses him out."

Jed stopped typing the email in mid-sentence. "Do you want me to keep him or not?" He saw from Mark's face that the CFO wasn't bluffing, and hastily added, "All right. But he's made a lousy job of negotiating Project Shield. I'm doing it myself, and I'll demand it's face to face with Andrew Aycliffe."

"Well, we're on the back foot," Mark cautioned. "Aycliffe's already told us to get lost."

"I'll send him a love letter." Jed was proud of this turn of phrase, another slice of humour he'd overheard and vowed to copy.

"You'll what?"

"I won't write it myself, of course. Let's get the customer communications manager, Matthew, to do it. Persuasion is his middle name."

The letter was a masterpiece. Jed regretted he had never had the opportunity to meet Andrew; he would like to put that right immediately, and suggested they enjoyed a VIP lunch and tickets for Aston Villa that weekend.

"Does that make sense to you?" Matthew asked, as Jed read the draft.

"I don't understand why I have to invite him to watch Aston Villa." Even as a student with little money, Jed had taken advantage of the rich cultural life on offer in Birmingham. Surely Andrew Aycliffe would prefer a concert or ballet performance?

"Aycliffe's well known to be a Villa supporter," Matthew explained. "Do you know much about the club?"

Jed did not, had in fact avoided knowing much about football at all, and gave Matthew the task of preparing a briefing pack on it.

The letter did not quite do the trick. Aycliffe sent an icy reply by email saying that he had a box at Villa Park and had made alternative arrangements to view the game with friends. Jed forwarded the email to Matthew, with a terse note ordering the man to report to his office at once.

"I wasn't expecting him to say no," Jed stated.

Matthew scratched his head. "Madrigal's based in Birmingham. Why don't you invite him to dinner at the best restaurant there?" he suggested.

"Very well." Even if Aycliffe didn't care for music, there was nothing to stop Jed extending his stay in Birmingham for a day or two. He might as well derive some enjoyment from the business trip, especially as his job was at risk if Project Shield collapsed. He told himself, like a mantra, that Project Shield must not fail.

"You can impress him with your newly acquired knowledge of Aston Villa," Matthew said.

An email was duly sent. Jed waited for Aycliffe's response. To his mounting irritation and dismay, hours, and then days, passed without one.

Chapter 11 Taylor's trip home

"Guess what?" Taylor said. "Martin Parsons wants us to do a photoshoot with our Airlite luggage. He's hired a photographer to snap us posing outside all the landmarks of Amsterdam."

Annie-Belle yawned. "I've done enough sightseeing," she objected. "Anyway, we're going home tomorrow, so there's no time."

"He's sending the photographer round now," Taylor said. "Do you think I should wear my red dress, or the green one?"

"You should wear a fur coat. That wind outside is blowing straight from the steppes," Annie-Belle said, adding, "I teach geography, so I know what I'm talking about."

Their room phone rang. "That'll be him." Taylor picked up the handset. "Nearly ready," she trilled. She decided on her green shift, and hastily changed into it, slicking on more lipstick and mascara.

There were two photographers, Dirk and Dan, both tall twentysomethings. Had it not been for her disappointing encounter with Boris, Taylor might have flirted with them. Dan in particular, with spiky brown hair and a wide grin, was very much her type. She consciously made an effort to build a rapport, though, as befitted a good journalist. "Rough weather, guys," she said.

Dark-haired Dirk shrugged. "We're used to it. Let's get the shoot over and done with, then we can go to a bar. Would you like that?"

"I certainly would. What is it you guys drink round here?"

"Anything," Dan replied.

Dirk laughed. "The local beer is Heineken. Have you been on a trip round the brewery? Many tourists do that."

"My friend doesn't drink," Taylor said.

"Then we'll have to show you how to do it. In fact, maybe we can do a few shots at the Heineken Experience later," Dan suggested. "We thought first we should take some pictures by the Royal Palace in the Dam Square, then a couple of other places. We can go for a drive in Dirk's car. Maybe Schiphol Airport, and after that, we'll find a windmill out in the countryside. Your American public think the Netherlands is full of windmills, I'm sure."

"They won't look so great against a grey sky," Taylor said, imagining the biting wind against her bare arms.

"Photoshop is my friend," Dirk replied. "No need to worry about the weather, Taylor. We'll be quick about it. Let me carry that Airlite baggage for you." He lifted the silvery suitcase easily. "My goodness, this is not weighty at all."

"A different story with Taylor's clothes in it, I expect," Dan winked.

They were as good as their word, clipping her hair out of her face, helping her to pose with the case and shooting photographs swiftly. The process took less than three hours, even after driving to the airport and a rather cute green and white windmill on the edge of a long, flat field.

"Do you think you could take a shot with my iPad here?" Taylor asked, pouting prettily by the windmill.

"Of course," Dirk said, accepting the iPad from her. "Oh dear, I think I pressed the wrong button. That man looks familiar. And the girl..." He gawped at Taylor.

"Give that back," Taylor yelled, cheeks flaming. She couldn't meet his eye.

"I think we really need that drink now," Dan said.

"I have another appointment," Dirk said, to Taylor's surprise and relief. "I'll drop you two at the old Heineken brewery."

"We can't carry the luggage around there," Dan said.

"I'll take it back to the hotel," Dirk assured them. "Now, let me adjust my satnav, and you'll be at the brewery in half an hour."

Taylor was dubious. "I've never liked beer."

"Trust me," Dan said. "Dutch beer actually tastes of something. Everybody likes it. Anyway Martin Parsons can treat us to a drink or two."

She did actually enjoy her beer on the Heineken tour, so much that she readily agreed to try more Dutch brands with Dan in a bar afterwards. It took a phone call from Annie-Belle to remind her that she ought to return to her hotel to pack.

Dan ordered a taxi and kissed her cheek. "Until next time," he said.

Taylor's suitcase had already been delivered to the hotel by Dirk and taken to her room. She slung her clothes into it, annoying Annie-Belle even more by proposing an early night.

The morning dawned stormy, with flurries of sleet lashing the hotel windows. Slightly hung over, Taylor dosed herself with coffee. She shook the reluctant Annie-Belle awake.

"What time is it?" Annie-Belle asked.

"Time to go to the airport. We have to be there three hours ahead, remember?"

Again, Annie-Belle's first action on arriving at the check-in desk was to request an upgrade.

"I'm afraid we can only offer this on a paid basis," the young man at the desk said.

"I think you should treat journalists better," Annie-Belle sniped.

"Sorry, I can't help. Let me check you in. Did you pack your cases yourselves?"

"Yes," Taylor said.

Annie-Belle nudged her. "I'm amazed everything fitted in yours, with all the samples you'd been given," she said.

The young man raised an eyebrow.

Taylor could see where the conversation was heading. "Samples of clothing," she said hurriedly. "I'm a fashion journalist – as well as a travel writer, obviously." She flashed her most brilliant smile at him.

"Why did you say that?" she asked Annie-Belle, when they were relaxing with strong Dutch coffee in the departure lounge.

Annie-Belle looked sheepish. "Aw, he knew it was a joke."

The flight passed uneventfully, mercifully free of bawling babies on this occasion. Taylor took full advantage of the in-flight movies and alcohol, constructing her own cocktails with the miniatures on offer. She was feeling happily intoxicated as the flight landed at JFK.

"I can't wait to get home," Annie-Belle confided. "Let's rush to the immigration area now and beat the lines."

"Whatever," Taylor agreed, still tipsy.

Annie-Belle rolled her eyes. "You're supposed to know all this stuff, Miss Travel Writer. Get power walking."

Their strategy worked, delivering them to the front of the immigration line within twenty minutes. Soon, they were collecting their cases from the carousel.

There was another queue ahead, this time to hand in their customs declaration forms. Taylor yawned.

"Just a moment." The customs and border protection agent was clearly speaking to Taylor. She smiled dreamily at him. He was youthful and cute, especially in his crisply ironed uniform.

"This is your bag, right?"

"Sure," Taylor said. Was he an idiot? Why would she be wheeling someone else's suitcase?

"Step this way please, miss. I need to inspect the contents."

Groggy from cocktails and the long, cramped journey, Taylor followed him meekly to a small, windowless room at the side of the baggage hall. Annie-Belle trailed behind with a bewildered look on her face.

"I know what this is about," Taylor said. "It's those sample clothes, isn't it? Whatever my friend said on checking in, there are only three garments and they were gifts, so I'm sure I'm not breaching my customs allowance."

"We'll see. Open the case."

Once she had unlocked it, he rifled through the carefully folded clothing in a desultory fashion, before taking a pen knife from his pocket.

"No!" Taylor exclaimed, remembering Mark's suspicions of drug smuggling. "There are no drugs anywhere in that case. You don't need to cut my clothes up."

Without a word, he applied the knife to the seemingly solid plastic interior of the suitcase's lid. The plastic peeled away, revealing a thin bubble wrap package taped behind it. With a single stroke of the blade, half a dozen sparkling stones clattered onto the lid.

"Diamonds," Annie-Belle gasped.

Taylor fainted.

Chapter 12 Boris' pictures

Boris awoke with a hangover. He'd been surprised, earlier in the week, to find himself unscathed by the heavy drinking on his stag party. Sunday's Buck's Fizz at the brunch was lightweight compared with the strong Belgian beers he'd imbibed over the rest of the weekend. He'd even downed four bottles returning on the Eurostar with Mark.

At least his credit card wasn't feeling the strain, as Mark had made liberal use of GardNet's travel budget for the whole party. Lee, he knew, was especially grateful for that, although it hadn't stopped him asking Boris for a loan and expressing irritation when it was refused.

Now it was Thursday, and at last, the hangover had hit him. Boris realised he must have stayed drunk since leaving Amsterdam, no doubt because he had topped up his alcohol level by splitting a bottle of dry white with Melissa over dinner each evening. Most of the wine had found its way into his glass, helping him forget his unease at his impending wedding.

His head throbbed. In his previous job, he would have phoned in sick. Knowing GardNet was desperate to secure its new call centre and might even have signed a deal with Madrigal overnight, he checked his emails. There was already a note from Mark warning him not to be late. Cursing, Boris dragged himself out of bed.

"Back to work, darling," he said to Melissa.

"Too early," she muttered. She usually woke at ten, practised for a couple of hours and then gave music tuition after lunch.

The man Melissa had said was a Pole, Szymon, was sitting at the reception desk downstairs. Having seen Boris, he stood up, yawned and stretched to his full height. "Good morning, sir. Have a nice day," he said to Boris, with exaggerated politeness.

Boris glowered up at him, and slammed the lobby door shut without replying.

There was no chance of a seat on the DLR, although Boris waited at the end of the platform and was rewarded with a slightly less crowded carriage in which to stand. He managed to lean against an interior wall, bracing himself with his feet so both hands were free to check emails.

Twenty emails had arrived since Mark's. He received a huge amount of spam. The message headed 'Pix' from a sender he did not recognise, A

Wright, was undoubtedly a prime example. Boris' finger slipped just as he was about to delete it, causing the message to open instead.

His own eyes, miniaturised, stared back from the screen of his iPad mini. There he was, nakedly clasping an equally nude Taylor. It was obvious what they were doing: one of the more inventive positions they had tried, less than a week before.

It was a photograph that he and his weekend companions had already seen, along with several others that Taylor had inadvertently distributed to the group. But how had A Wright acquired it, and why had he sent it to Boris again? Who else had received it?

Boris flushed with a toxic mixture of pride, shame and fear. He really had hit the big league, persuading a classy girl like Taylor to spend an adventurous night with him. Equally, he wished he'd asked all his stags to delete the photographs as soon as he knew that Taylor had circulated them to everyone. He should ask A Wright to refrain from disseminating them any further. Melissa must never find out.

Who was A Wright? He began to suspect Szymon. The man's exceptional cheerfulness would make sense if he were the culprit. He must have hacked into Boris' email account. The apartment complex had public wi-fi, and it was not unknown for Boris' iPad to connect to it automatically. When that happened, a hacker could exploit the obvious lack of security. Yet such an idea was fantastical. If Szymon were that IT literate, he would have a highly paid job in the City rather than his humble receptionist duties. Furthermore, Szymon would simply send photographs to Melissa if he wished to cause trouble.

Taylor, the photographs, A Wright and the polite reply Boris sent him, saying the pictures were a mistake and he would like them destroyed, were still buzzing in his head when Boris arrived at the office. Mark was waiting for him.

"Fancy a coffee?" Mark said. "Grab a meeting room, and I'll get the drinks."

Unlike Jed's huge room, and the antechamber where Valerie sat, GardNet's employees occupied an open plan space. Meeting rooms and soundproofed phone booths were provided for confidential discussions. On the plus side, there were machines that supplied more than palatable coffee, and quickly. Mark brought a couple of lattes within minutes.

"Yours has an extra shot, mate," Mark said. "You look like you need it. Still getting over the weekend? You need more practice."

"I've just received a photo I hope Melissa never sees."

Mark laughed. "More dirty pictures, eh? Who cares if she sees them; you can tell her the guy is Boris Johnson."

"Not that simple. I've got a birthmark here, and a mole there." Boris pointed at one of his arms. "They're not the only distinguishing marks. No, the real Boris is in the clear. She'd know it was me all right."

"Never mind. Back to work now. Project Shield."

"What's the latest?"

"Nothing. De nada. Zippo. Zilch. Andrew Aycliffe pulled the deal, and he won't respond to Jed's emails begging for a meeting."

"Who would?" Boris asked, in spite of himself. "Jed's hardly been to charm school. Why would you meet him if you didn't have to?"

"Exactly," Mark groaned. "Anyway, Jed's getting twitchy. He phoned me at six this morning."

"Doesn't that guy ever sleep?"

"Not much. He was already at the office, I understand. He's asked me – actually, no, he's told me – that we have to cut our costs in case we lose the Whitesmith contract. The first thing he said was, we won't need a tax accountant if the Madrigal deal falls through."

"That's hardly true," Boris said hotly. "How much tax do you want to pay?"

"As little as legally possible, and our investors think the same. I've told Jed that. You have my full support, but if I were you, I'd start looking around for something else. Treat it as an insurance policy."

"How's that going to look, if I've only been here for a couple of months and start seeking another job already?"

Mark clapped an open palm on his forehead. "Look mate, nobody would blame you. Everyone knows Jed's difficult. That's why we have to pay so much. Anyway, just put feelers out. Project Shield could still happen, and with it, your tasty bonus. Yum yum."

"Yum yum," echoed Boris. He had been promised £50,000 to deliver tax planning for Project Shield, in addition to his salary, which was itself twice what he had been earning before. He shivered. He'd been relying on the bonus to pay for the lavish wedding to which Melissa had committed him.

His plan to spend the morning calling headhunters was derailed by another email from the mysterious A Wright, requesting 'a modest donation of 250 bitcoins.' This, Wright said, would ensure no embarrassing photographs ended up in his fiancée's hands.

Boris felt nauseous. He realised he had no choice. 250 bitcoins was hardly modest. It amounted to about £3,000, but he had extended his credit card limit to meet the cost of his wedding, and could therefore afford to pay Wright. Melissa would never need to know. After a little research, Boris, briefly, had a digital wallet full of bitcoins. Shortly afterwards, he emailed Wright to say the virtual cash had been transferred in accordance with instructions.

Chapter 13 Andrew - after the interview

"It's your usual table, Mr Aycliffe, and your guest is already here."

"Thank you, Marta." He smiled at her. As was common in London, many of the club's staff were young Eastern Europeans, fresh faced and neat in their black uniforms. He liked them; they were sparky and ambitious. "How's your little boy?" he asked.

She glowed with pride. "Tomasz is really enjoying his school. Top of the class in English and maths."

"He does you credit," Andrew said.

Lianne rose from her seat for a hug and a peck on the cheek. Still slim and fair, she seemed much taller than he remembered. Andrew discounted the possibility of a late growth spurt, and looked at her feet. "Those are dominatrix shoes," he said. They were short black boots, with heels at least six inches high. She appeared to have no trouble standing in them, graceful as ever.

She brushed away his comment with a light laugh. "It's been a long time, Andrew," she said.

"I'm sorry," he admitted. "Work still comes first. It has to, now I'm CEO of Madrigal."

"You should pay attention to your fitness."

"I know," he said ruefully. "When I lived with you, I was the fittest I've ever been. I do make an effort now, though. I swim first thing every day when I'm at home. Up at 5.30 am, quick splash in the pool, and I'm ready for the day."

"Your own swimming pool?" Her sapphire eyes glinted. "OMG." She drew out the syllables, imbuing them with irony. "You really have made it."

"Two things, Lianne. Firstly – I had to put the hours in. Secondly, my house and its grounds, while exceptionally large and pleasant, are in Birmingham. For the same price, I could hardly buy a small terrace in Hampstead. Nor would I wish to." He felt it was worth making the point; it was her resentment at his so-called workaholism and his aching desire to escape London that had driven them apart seven years before.

Lianne grinned. "Yes, prices are mad in London. But I've decided to take the plunge and buy my flat in Hampstead, actually."

"You're a life coach now, aren't you? Not a personal trainer any more. You must be doing well."

They were interrupted by a waiter taking their order for lunch. Lianne asked for sparkling water as well.

"I take it that's acceptable to you, Andrew? Daddy always has lots of stories about long liquid lunches in the City, but I don't think our generation buys into that. I need a clear head for my clients this afternoon."

"I have work to do too."

"Until midnight in your case, I expect. Anyway. You asked about coaching. Of course, I loved being a personal trainer, but I couldn't make enough money out of it to have the lifestyle I wanted. Daddy was no help, saying that since the divorce, he had two extravagant wives to support and his children would have to fend for themselves. So I re-trained and re-branded and found some rich clients. One of them is a top executive at GardNet, for example."

Andrew leaned forward. "Not Jed Gardner, surely?"

Lianne laughed. "You know I can't tell you who my clients are, although no, it isn't Jed Gardner, actually. I thought you'd be interested. GardNet turned you down for a job, didn't they?"

"Just as well. I applied for a job in Birmingham, and within eighteen months, they'd closed their office there." He sipped his sparkling water. They had also offered him sparkling water at the GardNet interview seven years ago, he recalled. Fizzy water, fresh fruit and Haribos, obviously trying to seem hip and happy. That would never really work where Jed Gardner was concerned. His lack of empathy was too much in evidence.

The approach had come from a headhunter, Scott Georgeson.

"You want to leave London, don't you? I have a great opportunity for you; a really exciting tech start-up," Scott enthused. "They're a couple of guys, Jed and Mark, from the Midlands. Well, maybe they're not originally from the Midlands, but that's where they're based now. They used to work for another IT outsourcing company and they've just set up on their own."

"And how do I fit into this?" Andrew asked.

"They want a team leader who can progress to the next level."

Andrew agreed to an interview, and prepared for it by sounding out his contacts for information on both Jed Gardner and Mark Trelawney. He heard very little about Mark, who was a finance man, but plenty regarding Jed. It could be summarised in two words: evil genius. He was clearly the brains of the outfit, but known to have a volatile temper and to push his staff hard.

Beggars couldn't be choosers, though. Andrew was desperately homesick; not just for the streets of the busy, warm-hearted city of his birth, but for his extended family there. His father, who had enjoyed good health throughout Andrew's childhood, was becoming increasingly unwell. While Andrew wanted to progress in his career, to show his parents their support had been worthwhile, he wished most of all to live closer to them.

The interview was at GardNet's offices near Birmingham Airport. Luckily, Andrew knew the city well, and took Scott's assurances of a quick train journey from London with a pinch of salt. He left plenty of time to walk from Birmingham International train station or take a cab if it was raining.

Andrew's first impressions of GardNet were encouraging. There was a newish office, smartly clad in pale wood, and spacious inside. It was a welcome change from his workplace in London, where he and his team were packed like sardines in a small cubicle.

Mark Trelawney was waiting for him in the lobby. "Jed and I wanted to meet you ourselves, as we're a young business and every hire is important to us," he said. "Scott has recruited several excellent people for us, and he speaks very highly of you."

"Glad to hear it," Andrew said. "I hope I'll persuade you his confidence is justified. In my current role, I've doubled my team's output in six months and won a major new outsourcing client."

"You haven't improved your team's performance simply by increasing their hours, I hope?" Mark asked, a note of anxiety creeping into his voice.

"No," Andrew said, somewhat relieved that Mark thought this was important. "I work long hours myself; I'm a very driven individual, but I respect the work-life balance of my team members."

"You should get on well with Jed," Mark said cheerfully. "He's a very driven individual too. I'll take you to his office now, and we'll have the interview there."

Jed Gardner's office was situated at the top of the three storey building, with a fine view of trees, if not rolling countryside. Andrew was asked to sit at a meeting table while Mark found the CEO. "Help yourself," Mark said, gesturing to a tray of drinks and snacks.

A moment later, Mark returned. "Jed's tied up, I'm afraid," he apologised. "Look, I'll do the interview alone and catch up with him later."

The meeting with Mark appeared to go well. Mark was affable, listening with interest to Andrew's ideas for improving GardNet's business.

"Well, as far as I'm concerned, you've got the job," Mark said when Andrew departed an hour later. "I'll ask Jed to rubber stamp it, then we can make it official."

Andrew heard nothing for a week. He phoned Scott, only to learn that Jed had refused to make a job offer. In fact, he didn't even want to see Andrew.

"Get me in front of him and I'll change his mind," Andrew begged, confident that he would impress and even more anxious to leave London. By now, his father had been admitted to hospital. The prognosis was grim. Andrew had taken unpaid leave and was staying with his mother in the family home, a cramped terrace near the factory where his father worked.

"I can't make any promises," Scott warned. He secured a second interview for Andrew, however.

Jed must have been in his late twenties, hardly older than Andrew himself. Andrew extended his hand as he was ushered into the CEO's office.

Jed stayed in his chair, keeping his arms folded. "Sit down," he barked. "Really, this interview is highly inconvenient."

"Oh dear, have you been double-booked?" Andrew asked sympathetically.

Jed ignored him. "I've just looked at your CV," he said. "It's not exactly stellar, is it?"

Andrew stayed calm. "I've got a respectable track record," he said. "A 2:1 in Computer and Business Studies from Warwick, a history of providing IT services better and cheaper at Griffin, and winning new clients for them."

"Respectable doesn't cut it here," Jed said. "Why didn't you get a first? I like my programmes and systems to be perfect, and that means my people have to be perfect too."

Andrew was hardly surprised. Jed's perfectionism was well known. How commercial is that, Andrew thought. GardNet's service needed to be good enough for its clients, but not at an outrageous cost. He wondered briefly if GardNet was really the right place for him, then decided he would find a way to change Jed's perspective when he got the job. "You're the boss," he said.

Jed scowled. "That's not good enough," he said. "I need a team who will challenge me."

"Give me any problem you've got," Andrew said, "and I bet you'll like my solution."

"I don't have problems," Jed snarled. "I'm looking for people who can grow my business, not fix things that don't need it." He rose to his feet, and stared out of the window.

After what seemed an eternity, Andrew asked, "Do you have any other questions?"

"What, are you still here?" Jed said, to Andrew's amazement. "No, this interview's over."

"Goodbye. It was nice to meet you," Andrew said, habitually polite. Jed was silent. He pointed to the door.

Andrew had made his way straight to the hospital. By then, the family were keeping a vigil by his father's bedside. His father, who had seemed like a god, wise and immortal, during Andrew's childhood, had died within a couple of days. He was barely in his fifties.

"More water, Andrew?"

"Yes, please." Andrew was abruptly returned to the present moment and Lianne's puzzled expression. He blinked a tear from his eye. "Excuse me," he lied. "I must be starting a cold."

"Perhaps you're not as fit as you think," Lianne murmured.

Andrew ignored the bait. He couldn't banish Jed Gardner from his mind. "You may find this strange," he said. "I met Jed Gardner only once, but he made quite an impression on me." The man's rudeness still rankled. Worse, Andrew was convinced that Jed had maligned him to Scott Georgeson. Headhunters had stopped telephoning. It was purely by chance that he had discovered Madrigal was recruiting in Birmingham after that; a friend happened to mention it, and Andrew had applied direct to the company.

He continued his musings. "On the other hand, Gardner clearly has no idea who I am. He contacted me to tell me we'd never met, but he would like that to change. He's offered me VIP Villa tickets and a meal at Birmingham's best restaurant."

"Why?"

"You might well ask. Because I decided Madrigal should sell our call centre, and GardNet wanted to buy it. As soon as I found out the highest bidder by far was Jed Gardner's company, I took it off the market."

"To pay him back?"

"To give him sleepless nights at least. It's working. He keeps sending frantic emails asking for a meeting in Birmingham. Really, he hasn't a clue. I work in London two days a week, and stay here at my club; you know, there are rooms upstairs. He's based in London and he could easily ask for a meeting here. That would be far more convenient for him."

"Would you do it?"

Andrew laughed. "Probably not. Make him sweat. Although hell will freeze over before I have dinner with him."

"I won't breathe a word to my client," Lianne whispered theatrically.

"Quite right," Andrew said. "Although, if your client happens to tell you anything, I might like to know about it. I can't understand why GardNet is so interested in our call centre. It's a relatively modest one: 400 people in a northern town. GardNet already has a massive call centre in India, so why does it need ours?"

"I have no idea," Lianne said, "But I can find out for a fee."

"How much?"

"£30,000."

Andrew whistled. "No wonder you'll be buying property if you make that kind of money from your clients."

"Do you want the information or not?"

He stroked his beard. "It's a no-brainer."

"Leave it to me," Lianne said. "By the way, I'll be invoicing Madrigal for executive coaching services, and I'd like payment immediately."

"Lunch is still on me," Andrew said, "albeit it's more expensive than I expected."

"Pleasure doing business with you," Lianne said.

Chapter 14 Lianne's discovery

Lianne took a cab back to Hampstead. She didn't want to be late for Mark Trelawney. Humming, she decided to make certain changes to the session she'd planned. She reapplied makeup to flatter her pale skin, spritzed on heady perfume, and changed her clothes, dressing with particular care.

Her flat was already tidy to the point that it could have been a show home. There was not a speck of dust on the painted white floorboards. The cushions on the cream living room sofa were plumped and pristine. Every surface gleamed in the tiny lounge, bedroom, kitchen and cabin bathroom, although Mark wouldn't see most of the rooms. Lianne had made it clear from the start that her living and sleeping quarters were off limits to him.

The flat occupied half of the ground floor of a huge Arts and Crafts mansion, a rather imposing property standing proud on a hill near the heath. What made the flat special for Lianne was its secret, which she had only unmasked once she had moved in and ripped up the swirly orange carpet that had covered the floor in the lobby. There, hidden now by a fluffy white rug, was the trapdoor that led to stone steps down to a cellar running the full length and width of the house.

The cellar had no other access. Now she had offered to buy the apartment from her landlord, her lawyers had found out what she had long suspected: that the brick vaults she had discovered were legally part of her flat. Her landlord evidently did not know or care; her flat was no more expensive than others in the area without extra storage space.

In truth, the cellar, a series of vaulted rooms with a flagstone floor, was probably just the foundations of the house. It had inspired new possibilities for Lianne, however, and in turn, she had introduced them to her clients.

Mark Trelawney looked every inch the accountant, from his Austin Reed suit to the silver-framed spectacles on his nondescript face. In her personal training days when she worked mostly in gyms on the fringes of the City, she had seen hundreds of men who resembled him: slim, of medium height, with mousy hair, green eyes, square jaws, mouths set in a neutral position. She wondered now what secrets they held behind the anonymous facades they presented the world. Blending into the crowd gave them safety, of course. If Mark ever committed a major crime, she was sure the police would never find him among his clones.

"What is your plan today, Mistress?" he asked, hanging his jacket and laptop bag on a hook by the door.

"That's for me to know and you to find out, wretch." She softened a little, and said, "Can't you guess?"

"A sporting theme?" He was looking lasciviously at her legs and breasts.

She caught his eye and sneered. "You're not good enough to touch me, and don't you forget it. And it's 'Miss' to you, Trelawney Minor, at least for today. Make sure you behave, boy."

"You're my gym teacher."

It had taken him long enough to guess. She was wearing shiny black leather shorts, a skimpy white singlet, a whistle on a lanyard round her neck and those stilettoed boots. "Yes?"

"Miss," he said.

"Good. You'll be sorry you forgot to say that, Trelawney Minor. I'm going to punish you later." She let him digest the implications, then said briskly, "Remove all your clothes except your underwear, and we'll go to the gym to use the equipment."

"Yes, Miss."

As always, he did as he was told. Meanwhile, Lianne pushed the rug to one side and opened the trapdoor. She had taken the precaution of running a fan heater in the cellar all morning, so the subterranean rooms were not too cold. Although she didn't care whether Mark suffered from goose pimples, she valued her own comfort.

When he was standing before her, wearing only underpants and socks, Lianne blew her whistle. "Down the steps, Trelawney Minor. We will use the horse today."

"I prefer the cross, Miss."

Lianne blew her whistle again. "Insolent boy! You will be severely chastised for that remark. Now, move it or I'll kick you down those steps."

"Yes, Miss."

Mark meekly entered the cellar and lay prone on the spanking horse, a padded bench with a slightly lower kneeling platform, and cuffs for his wrists and ankles. Lianne snapped the cuffs firmly shut, removed his spectacles and placed a leather hood over his head. He could breathe and speak, but he would see nothing.

"You've been a bad boy, Trelawney Minor, haven't you?"

58

"Yes, Miss. Sorry, Miss."

"Sorry isn't good enough. You know what's going to happen, don't you?"

"Yes, Miss."

"No, you don't know." Lianne took a leather bullwhip from a selection neatly hanging on the wall. She cracked it three times before replacing it and taking a wooden paddle. She rapped his shoulders smartly.

"You like that, don't you, boy?"

Mark was silent.

Lianne increased the frequency of her blows, hitting Mark's upper back and then moving on to his lower back and buttocks.

"I can't hear you."

"Yes, Miss."

"You're not supposed to like it," she exclaimed, injecting a note of derision. "I'll have to deal with you severely."

Once more, she took the bullwhip and flicked it lightly across his shoulder blades. There, it wouldn't bruise and she was careful not to cut his skin. No one would know that Mark's sessions with her were not executive coaching as he claimed.

"I think, like all bad boys, you have dirty secrets," she said. "You're going to tell me about them."

"Yes, Miss."

"Well?

"I tried to seduce a woman in Amsterdam, Miss."

"Oh?" Lianne was interested. As far as she knew, Mark was happily married to Helena. "You tried, did you? Hmm. You did not succeed, then, boy. That makes your petty adultery worse." She whipped him with more force, still restricting her activities to the bony areas of his upper back.

Mark moaned with pleasure. "Miss, I didn't mean to seduce anyone. I was just helping a colleague."

"Why is this colleague so important to you? Was it Jed Gardner?"

He was silent. Lianne didn't care about bruising him now. Let him explain to his wife how he spent his free time in both Amsterdam and London. She moved her lashes to his lower back. Beads of sweat were forming on Mark's skin, a musky scent rising from him.

"I think it was Jed Gardner, and you're afraid of him. But I'll give you something to be scared about." Lianne was proud of her imagination.

With only a taxi journey in which to plan the session, she was sustaining their role play remarkably well. She pulled Mark's underpants down to expose his buttocks, cracked the whip again and applied it vigorously to them.

He yelped. Luckily, the cellar walls were thick. Apart from Lianne, nobody would hear him.

"Yellow," Mark gasped, adding, "Miss."

"What are you and Gardner plotting, Trelawney Minor?" She swapped the bullwhip for a riding crop, less noisy but even more powerful.

"Yellow," Mark said again, his voice rising to a shout. He wriggled, pulling at his shackles.

"Don't forget who I am, wretched boy."

"Miss."

"That's better. Now, I'm going to beat you some more. Don't expect mercy from me, boy."

She hit with him such energy that the spanking horse trembled.

"Ouch! Red, Miss, red."

'Red' meant she should stop at once. "You don't really mean that, boy, do you? I know you want some more." She rapped his naked bottom again.

Mark appeared terrified. He screamed; a harsh, animal sound. Lianne stifled a yawn. While she didn't derive enjoyment from his fear and pain, nor did she care much. Apart from a couple of gems whom she held in genuine affection, she felt nothing but contempt for her customers.

"Red," Mark shouted again.

"What?"

"Miss," said Mark.

She reduced the pressure of the crop. "Maybe I won't punish you quite so much, Trelawney Minor."

"Still red, Miss. I've had enough." He was almost sobbing.

"You need a cold shower, boy."

They blinked as they emerged into daylight from the cellar. Lianne handed him a towel and he disappeared through a sliding door into her bathroom, a closet-like room opposite the front door.

Mark had revealed nothing of interest during the session. He would have divulged secrets if she had pressed him, she was sure, but she couldn't afford to excite his suspicion. Hastily, Lianne rifled through his case. With no time to boot up Mark's laptop while he was in the shower,

60

she searched for papers that would explain why Jed Gardner wanted Madrigal's call centre.

There was a sheaf of documents in a plastic wallet. It was too risky to pilfer them. Lianne read the news of Whitesmith's ultimatum and committed it to memory as best she could.

She had expected Mark to have a hot shower – after all, the role play was over – but he returned, teeth chattering and eyes shining. Hearing him unlock the bathroom door, she stuffed the papers back in his case. She could only hope she had left everything in order.

"That was the best session we've ever done, Mistress," he observed.

While his words and voice were respectful, Lianne detected a reptilian coldness in his gaze. She responded in kind. "Get out, you worm," she said, curling her lip. "And before you come back, make sure all my fees are paid. My last invoice hasn't been settled. What are you going to do about it?"

"I'm so sorry, Mistress. I'll phone my accounts department now," Mark said. "I'm their boss, so they'd better jump to it." He jabbed at his mobile. "Hello, Christina. My executive coach tells me she has an invoice outstanding with us. Can you sort it, please?"

Lianne barely had time to spray disinfectant all over her bathroom and ring Andrew before her next client arrived. Unlike Mark, this man was one of her favourites. He was readily admitted to the inner sanctum of her flat, largely because he liked nothing better than donning a French maid's uniform and doing all of her housework.

Chapter 15 Andrew's response

Andrew recognised Lianne's number immediately. "What news?" he asked.

"GardNet will lose at least one client if it can't buy the call centre," she said. "They have one month to do it, or Whitesmith will leave."

Andrew whistled. "Whitesmith is their oldest, and biggest, client," he said. He stroked his beard, slightly puzzled that Whitesmith's contract gave them the power to walk. It was industry practice to specify services down to the tiniest detail, with swingeing penalties if either side breached the agreement in any way. GardNet surely had the power to locate their call centres wherever they chose? They had been using one in Birmingham when they began to work for Whitesmith. Presumably the latter had acquiesced when they moved the activity to Bangalore.

None of this was Lianne's concern, he knew. He thanked her for the information, asked her to send him an invoice, and convened a meeting of his executive directors. There were only three of them, all based in Madrigal's small London office in Shoreditch, so the discussion was short.

"You all know about our South Shields division," he told them. "I decided that no one was offering enough, and withdrew the call centre division from the market. Confidentially, I understand that GardNet is under commercial pressure to acquire a call centre within the next month. That means they can be persuaded to pay a premium price. Therefore, we should recommence negotiations with them."

There was a general murmur of agreement. Andrew continued. "Just one point. Jed Gardner is leading negotiations from his side, and I suggest I do the same for Madrigal. Any objections?"

He was sure Ruby wouldn't mind, and predictably, nobody else was keen to meet the notoriously short-tempered Jed Gardner.

Andrew asked his PA to arrange a call with Gardner. By the time she left for the day, there had been no response from Gardner's office.

"Don't forget, I'm in Birmingham tomorrow," he said. His car was waiting for him in the underground car park below his office. When the traffic eased, perhaps at eight or nine o'clock, he would drive back to the second city. As with his early morning swim, Andrew found driving a great stress reliever. Last summer, he had treated himself to the ultimate birthday present: a red Audi R8 Spyder Quattro convertible. Although the icy winter weather was not conducive to open top trips, he still took a childish thrill in the car's swift acceleration.

He'd spent the previous night at his club, so it was a pleasure for Andrew to wake in his own bed next morning. It was still dark by the time he had swum, breakfasted and driven to his office in the centre of Birmingham. Nevertheless, he already had an email from Jed Gardner saying he had tried to call a few minutes ago.

Gardner had left his mobile phone number, so Andrew called him back. He was curious to hear the reaction of the man who had cut him dead seven years before.

Jed picked up the phone with a single, barked, "Gardner."

"It's Andrew Aycliffe."

"Ah, Andrew. Good to hear from you." There was a pause, then slowly, as if reading from a script, Gardner said, "Aston Villa did rather well this weekend."

"I was there," Andrew said.

"You – must be pleased."

"Delighted." Andrew decided to cut to the chase. "You want to buy our northern call centre. I took it off the market because the money wasn't right. I'm not in a hurry to sell. It's a profitable division."

"It isn't your core business."

Andrew yawned. He frequently heard this comment from his fellow directors and from the large investment funds who had bought shares in Madrigal when it floated on the London Stock Exchange. He always gave them the same answer, and he repeated it to Gardner. "It makes money, it takes up very little of my time, and I won't sell it unless the price is right. We had exploratory talks, I felt no one was offering enough, and I decided I would best serve my shareholders' interests by keeping the call centre."

"I can find more money."

"That's good to know. I think you and I should meet to discuss it."

"You've sacked your negotiating team, have you?" Gardner said. "I had to tell mine to step aside as well. Completely useless. You'll be glad to hear that I want to deal with this myself."

"As will I." Andrew was not warming to the man.

"Let's meet. How about tomorrow?" Gardner sounded eager. "Or any other day this week. This weekend, even."

"I'm afraid that's out of the question," Andrew lied. "My diary is booked solid for a full month ahead, including weekends."

"It really will be a pleasure to meet you," said Gardner, again sounding like an actor learning a script. "Couldn't we do it a bit sooner?"

"Not possible." Andrew was enjoying himself.

"I wanted a quick deal. That's why I'm prepared to pay more. If you can't sell quickly, I'll go elsewhere."

"That's a risk I'm prepared to take." Andrew knew there was no risk at all. GardNet really needed the call centre. There were no similar businesses available for sale. He had every intention of selling to Gardner, but only for an exorbitant price. His best chance of securing that lay in making Gardner wait until Whitesmith's deadline was upon him. He smiled, savouring the opportunity to teach Gardner a lesson.

Chapter 16 Jed – after the interview

The day dawned crisp and cold, with condensation on the arched windows of Jed's flat in St Pancras Chambers. His meeting with Andrew Aycliffe was scheduled for eleven o'clock, less than 48 hours before Whitesmith's deadline expired. First, as usual, he took an early cab to his workplace.

Mark was yawning as he entered Jed's office at 7 am. "Sorry, the baby was screaming at four," he said.

"Oh?" Jed had learned this was a useful phrase when he believed another person's private life was their own concern, but judged it inadvisable to say so.

"No alarm clock required this morning," Mark added. "I thought you'd like a double espresso to start the day, Jed." He handed over a plastic cup of hot, black liquid.

Jed accepted it gratefully, noticing that Mark had lined up two lattes for himself. "You really are tired, Mark."

"I still wanted to see you before you went to Madrigal's office."

"The meeting isn't there. It's at their lawyer's."

"Whatever," Mark said. "Listen, Jed, I was horrified to find out from Raj yesterday that you were planning to go there alone. He'd usually take a lawyer like Barney with him, to make sure nobody tried to make him sign up to something we didn't want."

"Aycliffe insisted I was alone, meeting him man to man."

"It sounds like a duel, with smoking guns at dawn. Jed, don't fall for his tricks. He's a player. Do you think Andrew Aycliffe won't have lawyers around if you're meeting at their premises? These delaying tactics he's used are a negotiating ploy as well. Just to make sure he doesn't slip any stupid terms and conditions into the agreement, I've had Barney draft a standard contract to buy the call centre. Here it is." Mark handed Jed several printed pages. "I've emailed it to you as well," he added.

"What does it matter?" Jed shrugged. "We have to do this deal, and quickly, so the only issue is the price."

"All you have to do is slot in the price here, and sign it, when you reach an accord," Mark said. "Jed, the most we can afford to pay is £60m, OK? Any more than that, and I've calculated Project Shield is earnings negative. We'd be better off losing Whitesmith as a client, unappealing though that prospect is."

"What about Boris' tax scheme? Won't that help?"

"I don't want to build it into the projections we give GardNet's shareholders. It's not certain to work."

"Why are we employing him then?" Jed was outraged. "He's nothing but trouble."

"Boris seems to have got off on the wrong foot with you," Mark said. "From where I'm sitting, he's working hard and adding value, so what's winding you up? It's all about the girl, isn't it?"

Mark was far too perceptive. "Not at all," Jed said. He recognised that Mark was probably right, but nothing would make him admit it.

"Good," Mark said, looking relieved. "I wouldn't dream of advising you on affairs of the heart, Jed, but at least trust me on financial matters. No, the tax scheme may not work, but it probably will. The cost of employing Boris to set it up is peanuts compared with the potential benefit. I don't need to tell you that both Whitesmith and Madrigal could bring this business to its knees if we're not careful, though. If Whitesmith walks away, we're toast. Ditto if we overpay Madrigal. You're treading on a tightrope today, Jed. Let me come with you. It'll help to have an extra voice beating Aycliffe down."

"Which bit of 'I will be alone' do you not understand?" Jed wished Mark would listen.

"Whatever you agreed with Aycliffe, pretend you forgot," Mark suggested.

Irritated, Jed nevertheless agreed to share a cab to Madrigal's lawyers' office. It occupied the whole of a six storey glass lozenge on the edge of the City, an area of largely red brick buildings with the names of long dead wholesalers and factories stencilled on their walls. Now they were loft apartments, swanky gentlemen's clubs and expensive offices. Jed and Mark easily negotiated their first hurdle, as both were given security passes at the door and directed up an escalator which pulsed with blue light at their feet.

"Funky," Mark murmured.

They arrived in another lobby, this time staffed by immaculately groomed young women sitting at a curved glass reception desk. There, despite Mark's charm, he was unable to gain admittance. There was a visitor's badge reserved for Jed Gardner only, and the polite and pretty receptionist had express instructions to allow Jed alone to enter.

"Never mind," Mark said. "I'll see you back at the ranch. Call me if you have any questions or problems, all right?" He waved and winked as Jed was led through a glass security gate to the meeting rooms beyond.

Lawyers held no terror for Jed. He had met plenty in his professional career. All, like the man who was ushering him to see Aycliffe, had a public school veneer and a desire to make small talk to which Jed was completely impervious. Equally, Jed had seen many meeting rooms like the one to which he was escorted: a windowless cube with white walls, a grey carpet, and half a dozen chrome and leather chairs surrounding an oblong black glass table.

Andrew Aycliffe, seated near the door, rose to his feet. He was slightly shorter than Jed, slim, with dark wavy hair waxed back. Apart from his wide blue eyes, his face, and all expression in it, was hidden by a trim beard. Jed remembered Eleanor saying that the eyes were the window to the soul. He hoped Aycliffe's would be easy to read.

"Pleased to meet you at last," Jed said, extending a hand. He had spent time preparing some phrases to use at the meeting, including a few positive comments about Aston Villa.

"Likewise," said Aycliffe. His handshake was firm. An emotion - excitement or annoyance; if only it were possible to tell – flickered briefly in his blue eyes. He gestured to the end of the table. "They've provided coffee and sandwiches. Please tuck in."

"I've heard a lot about you," Jed said, filling a cup to the brim with black coffee and sitting across the table from Madrigal's CEO. "You've enjoyed a lot of success, very young."

"I joined Madrigal at the right time, certainly," Aycliffe said. "It was owned by the Armstrong family, and it was an excellent business, but they had no plans for growth. Once they decided to sell it on the London Stock Exchange, they recruited me to manage the project and rapidly realised I'd make a great chief executive." He smiled, seemingly in a good mood. "Since then, Madrigal's profits have tripled."

Jed nodded. He was unnerved, finding it difficult to concentrate on everything Aycliffe was saying. He had not expected the man to be so chatty. "You want to stick to developing products rather than manning a call centre," he said, hoping to return Aycliffe's focus to the deal on the table.

"I'll come to that," Aycliffe said. "I have done well, and Madrigal's shareholders have done even better. You will be aware that we don't throw money away. Our headquarters are in Birmingham. There's a small London office, near Silicon Roundabout. We bought it cheaply and did it up. Our operations are largely in the UK, but we avoid high-cost areas. That's how I can afford to wait for a good price for our call centre in South Shields. No, I don't really need it anymore; I'd prefer to stick to offering end user support for our own products only, but I may still decide not to sell it. I hear on the grapevine that Whitesmith would like a call centre on Tyneside. Perhaps I'll do a deal with them."

Jed's initial wrath at what he perceived as Aycliffe's criticism of GardNet's expensive London office gave way to shock at the mention of Whitesmith. "Where have you heard that?" he asked sharply.

"Industry gossip," Aycliffe shrugged, his eyes betraying nothing. "What's your view of it?"

"I don't have one," Jed blustered.

"Come on, Jed. Whitesmith's your biggest client. You must be close enough to them to know what they're thinking."

Jed's mind was racing furiously. Aycliffe obviously knew he was onto something. Who could have told him, and was the knowledge widespread? The leak might have come from Whitesmith itself, rather than GardNet. Speculation was pointless, he decided. He would do his best to secure a deal with Madrigal before Whitesmith bought the call centre direct. "What Whitesmith thinks is irrelevant," he said. "I want to buy that business. We offered you £30m before; I think we can stretch to another £5m. Mark Trelawney, my CFO, has the bank facility in place."

Aycliffe was silent.

"Do we have a deal?" Jed asked.

"No, I don't think so," Aycliffe said.

"£40m." Jed added, "Anything more, and I must consult my shareholders." This was by no means true, but he hoped it would provoke a quick decision to sell.

"Well, you'll have to, then," Aycliffe said, to Jed's disappointment. "Our South Shields division is worth at least twice that amount. I've told you before, I'm not giving it away. I have a duty to Madrigal's shareholders."

"I promised you I'd find more money, and I have," Jed said. "It would be too much of a stretch to double it."

"Then we have nothing more to say to each other," Aycliffe said, maintaining his poker face. "I'll give Whitesmith a call this afternoon."

Jed imagined a life without his career at GardNet: the plush office, Valerie's sixth sense for supplying espressos, the intellectual satisfaction of solving business-critical IT problems. A huge black void stretched ahead for the rest of his life. "Wait," he said. "How does £50m sound?"

"Too little," Aycliffe said dismissively.

"I can pay £60m. That's my limit." He sensed sweat building on the palms of his hands, prickling his armpits underneath his crisp white cotton shirt.

"That's still nowhere near enough," Aycliffe said.

"£65m," Jed said. GardNet could surely squeeze a few drops of extra value from the call centre. Raj had said Whitesmith would pay a higher service fee, hadn't he? They could cut wages in South Shields as well. Mark had virtually intimated that the locals would work for a pittance.

"You're having a laugh."

"£70m." Jed knew sweat was beginning to trickle down his face; his fringe and sideburns felt damp, plastered against his skin. He took a deep breath. Brooks' tax planning would just have to pay for the difference, whatever Mark said. Mark was always cautious in financial matters, anyway; his £60m upper limit was almost certainly too pessimistic.

Aycliffe sighed. "I as good as said it was worth £80m. I won't take less."

"Then £80m it is," Jed said. Mark might not be happy, but this deal was essential for both to keep their jobs. He felt as he might have done thirty years before, when he had disobeyed Eleanor's instructions not to wander out of the garden to look at the railway line. Although no harm had been done, her reaction had been shocked and sorrowful. Jed suspected Mark's response would be similar.

Aycliffe offered him a hand to shake. "Yes," he said. There was no smile. Madrigal's CEO was still curiously unreadable.

"I have a contract for you to sign," Jed said, giving Aycliffe the draft agreement that Mark had supplied that morning. "All we have to do is slot in the price, here. I'll write it in now."

Aycliffe scanned the pages swiftly. His eyes darkened. "This is completely unacceptable. Madrigal never gives warranties and indemnities."

"It's usual practice, surely?" Jed pointed out. He had done enough deals to know. "We'd normally have warranties that the call centre's operating to acceptable service levels, paying its staff on time and so on, and indemnities that would make you reimburse us if that weren't the case."

"I'm not signing this." Aycliffe ripped the document in half, and threw the torn pages on the table. "I'll ask my lawyer to draft a simpler version. No warranties and indemnities." He took a smartphone from his pocket. "Hello, Adam? Can you bring in a sale contract, as we discussed previously? Yes, the price is £80m. You'll be five minutes? Fine. Bring someone with you; we'll need two witnesses."

The man who had ushered Jed to the meeting room arrived, with a female colleague. Aycliffe took great pains to sit beside Jed, reading each line of the two page contract with him.

"What's this?" Jed asked. "You said there were no warranties and indemnities. This contract forces me to keep staff employment terms the same in South Shields, and to recognise a union."

"We're not giving warranties and indemnities," Aycliffe said.

"Then why must I give any undertakings to you? I don't have a single unionised facility across the whole of GardNet, and I don't intend to start."

"In that case, our deal's off," Aycliffe said, again betraying no emotion.

"Are you some kind of Marxist?" Jed exploded.

"These guys in South Shields are part of the Madrigal team. I want to ensure they're treated decently once they transfer to you. It's in your interests to look after them, anyway. They give great customer service. Whitesmith would love them."

He was talking about Whitesmith still. Jed felt he was treading on eggshells. How much did Aycliffe know, and how? "Why the requirement to pay you from a UK bank account?" Jed asked.

"Madrigal's a listed company, and we care about our reputation. We don't want to be party to any exotic Cayman Islands tax schemes you may want to use."

"How dare you," Jed said, realising it was unwise to admit that a tax scheme was in prospect. "GardNet deals with both the tax authorities and its employees in an honourable fashion. I don't see why I should sign a document that implies we would not. Call any other bidder you like. I bet you won't secure as good a price."

"I'm a betting man, Jed," Aycliffe said. A half-smile played on his lips, almost buried beneath his beard.

"If you would do those things, as you say," Adam, the lawyer, interrupted, "why is it a problem to sign an agreement that formalises them?"

Jed nodded. His adrenaline was still flowing. With a steady hand, he signed and dated the foot of the second page. Andrew Aycliffe added his signature and passed the document to the lawyers to sign as witnesses.

Jed sighed with relief. At last, there could be no doubt that GardNet would retain Whitesmith as a client. The company's future was assured.

"I look forward to receiving the cash," Aycliffe said. "You have two days to raise it."

Jed was about to reply, but Aycliffe clearly wasn't finished.

"I want to speak privately with Jed," he said to his two lawyers. They left the room, Adam clutching the signed contract in his hand.

"Yes?" Jed was puzzled.

"We've met before, actually," Aycliffe said.

"I'm sorry, I have no recollection of it. Where was it – the terraces of Aston Villa, perhaps?" Jed knew it couldn't have been; he had never attended a football match in his life.

"It was GardNet's offices in Birmingham, which you later saw fit to close. Unlike Madrigal, you seem to have decided a lavish head office in London is more your style now. You interviewed me for a job. You turned me down."

"That's regrettable," Jed said. He had no idea what Aycliffe was talking about.

"Most regrettable," said Aycliffe. "The rejection hurt a little, naturally. What really stung me was the way you treated me during our meeting. You asked me no more than three or four questions, then dismissed me like an inconvenient fly being swatted away."

Jed fidgeted. Despite hating interviews, he had conducted hundreds, all merging into a single blurred memory from which Andrew Aycliffe was unaccountably absent. It was a pity GardNet had missed out on Aycliffe's talents – his track record at Madrigal was undeniably impressive - but that was hardly any concern of Aycliffe's.

"I'm sure you trashed me to the headhunter afterwards," Aycliffe said. "You could have totally wrecked my career."

"I really don't remember," Jed said, mystified. This was not at all relevant to Project Shield. He looked impatiently at the clock, hoping Aycliffe would take the hint.

"You know," Aycliffe said, his smirk easy to see despite his beard, "I would have sold that call centre to anyone else for less. It's worth £35m, maybe a bit more. Your finance man, Mark, should have told you that. A decent enough guy, I recall, but obviously stupid to let you overspend." He shook his head. "Just wait until I tell my board, and even better, when we announce the news to the stock market. Madrigal's share price will go through the roof."

"No," Jed said. "We can rewrite the agreement if the price is clearly wrong."

"You can't," Aycliffe crowed. "You signed on the line. I checked the legal position with Adam before our meeting. A bad bargain is still a bargain in the eyes of the law." He laughed again. "Our meeting's over, I believe."

Aycliffe offered his hand. Almost mechanically, Jed was about to shake it in farewell. At the last second, he drew back.

"We've both done what we came here for," Jed said. "Where's your lawyer?"

Adam was summoned to show Jed out, also pressing into his hand an envelope which Jed was assured contained a copy of the contract. The lawyer was more subdued than before. Perhaps he finally appreciated Jed disliked small talk.

Jed rarely experienced shame or guilt, but now, both assailed him. He was indifferent to Aycliffe's colourful tale of the job interview. Until that point, he had rather admired Aycliffe's single-minded focus in negotiating, but the story showed Aycliffe was either a fantasist, or should man up. In any event, even if he had refused a job to Aycliffe, it had been the right decision. Agreeing on £80m for Project Shield was another matter. He had been foolish. Would his flat have to be sold to pay for it?

Although cold, the day was still bright. Jed realised he hadn't taken a single one of the offered sandwiches, and he now felt too nauseous to stop anywhere for lunch. He walked to Bishopsgate and hailed a cab.

Mark took one look at him and asked, in a worried tone, what had happened.

"The good news is, we're buying the call centre," Jed said, attempting levity. "The bad news is, Aycliffe somehow knew Whitesmith was interested, and he wouldn't give it away. It's costing £80m."

All the colour drained from Mark's face.

"Here's the agreement," Jed said, passing to Mark the photocopied sheets that Adam had given him as Jed left his office.

"Ouch," said Mark, still visibly reeling. "No warranties for us, and we're obliged to recognise a union. I don't like it. And what's this requirement for a UK bank account?"

"Aycliffe insisted. He didn't want us doing a tax scheme. I guess we don't need a tax manager after all."

"I think we do," said Mark. "As it happens, Andrew Aycliffe can't stop Boris. We can route funds through Luxembourg, Switzerland, Timbuktu or wherever Boris likes before sending them back to the UK. Our tax planning won't be affected, and at this price, we'll be relying on it now to sell the deal to our shareholders. It had better work, mate. Seriously, Jed, Boris is the most important man in this company right now."

It was Jed's turn to blanch.

Chapter 17 Boris' big day

Valentine's Day dawned, and with it a frantic stream of emails from the lawyers who were helping Boris with the Project Shield tax structure. He had stayed overnight in the country house hotel outside Brighton where he was to be married. It was grand, stuffy and dreadfully dull, but he was glad Melissa had chosen it over costlier alternatives involving the old Naval College in Greenwich and a cruise down the Thames. Predictably, her parents had chosen to let him finance the wedding alone: 'That's modern life, isn't it?' her father had told him.

As was proper, Melissa had spent her last night as a spinster at her parents' house in the town. Boris groaned, wondering how he would keep her family and his apart. More particularly, as his parents were dead, his main concern was preventing his older sister from speaking to Melissa's relatives. Like his late parents, Marianne was convinced that Melissa was a gold digger; in her Yorkshire way, she was forthright in expressing her opinions. He resolved to have a quiet word with his best man.

Boris tapped away at his tablet, glad he had resisted his friends' calls for another stag celebration the previous evening. The work took his mind off the dull day ahead and a tedious future of family life in suburbia. With plenty of coffee and a large breakfast to give him energy, he was just about keeping pace with the flurry of emails. With a start, he realised he had nearly overlooked another message from A Wright.

It had arrived overnight, at around 2 am. 'I would be most grateful to celebrate your wedding day with a gift of 185 bitcoins, very truly yours, A Wright.' There was another picture attached, as if the blackmailer were reminding Boris just how many incriminating photographs existed. It was the fourth request for money, always polite and accompanied by a photograph he would never want Melissa to see. Boris had paid the preceding three, which had arrived at roughly weekly intervals. Each asked for slightly fewer bitcoins than last time. This was not due to any generosity on Wright's part; it was a simple fact that the virtual currency was appreciating against its real life counterparts. The transfers always cost Boris around £3,000.

Feeling sick, he prepared to make yet another payment. When would this end, and how? He still suspected Szymon, and had fantasised about slipping a knife in the man's back, even researching murder methods on the internet. All that had stopped him was the CCTV throughout the public areas of the Greenwich apartment block, and a wavering uncertainty that he had identified the right culprit.

His phone began to ring. It was Mark.

"Can you talk, mate?"

"Yes," Boris assured Mark. "I'm not at the church yet, but I'm about to don morning dress."

"We need you back at the office. Jed's thrown a wobbler."

"That's taking liberties, and you know it, Mark. It's my wedding day." Despite his reliance on the forthcoming bonus to pay for both the wedding and A Wright's demands, Boris felt justified in setting boundaries.

"How about tomorrow?"

"It's my honeymoon. A short break in Paris. Remember? I had to cancel Bali." That had actually worked quite well for Melissa; the Orchestra of London had secured a gig at the Mansion House the following week, which would have been impossible if they had taken the two week honeymoon she initially wanted.

Mark made a sucking noise. "Look, you need to be available on your phone, OK? At all times."

"Except during the wedding ceremony, yes," said Boris, forgetting all about Wright in his hurry to respond to half a dozen emails from Jed that had just filled his inbox. Once they were answered, he had barely time to shave and dress before his best man and ushers arrived.

"Ready, Desperate Dan?" Boris asked.

His best man, Danny, grinned. "I've got the ring if that's what you mean," he said. "What an odd couple we make. I bet you're glad we're not marrying each other today."

"Yes, not being that way inclined," Boris said. Danny was abnormally tall, and towered above him even more than most of his friends. He had a medical condition called gigantism. Still, as both had met on their first day at school and been buddies ever since, Danny was the natural choice for best man.

"I never thought Boris was inclined to marry at all," Danny said, nudging Lee, one of the ushers.

"Especially not when he pulled that little redhead in Amsterdam," Lee said, a roguish glint in his eye. "Nice of her to share the dirty pictures with us."

"You should have shown them to your wife," Danny suggested to Lee. "Give her some ideas."

"Her only ideas involve spending my cash," Lee groaned.

"You didn't buy that new car for her, though, did you?" Danny asked. "That number plate's got your name on it."

"A new car with a personal plate?" Boris was curious. "How could you afford it? You only came on the stag because Danny found a two for one deal." Not only that, but Lee had recently pleaded for a loan just to meet household expenses.

"I suppose you had a Christmas bonus," Danny said.

Boris doubted it. Lee's employers, a small firm of accountants, were notoriously mean.

"My father-in-law lent me ten grand," Lee said, adding hurriedly, "but don't tell my wife, because he didn't want her to know. Truly, he didn't."

"That's more than my new father-in-law has ever done," Boris said ruefully, uncertain that he believed his friend. "By the way, can you keep my sister away from Melissa's rellies? They'll likely come to blows if you can't."

There was a chapel in the hotel grounds, a photogenic Victorian Gothic building. Boris and Danny made their way to the altar, accepting congratulations from guests as the chapel filled. Marianne, bosomy in a red coat that reminded Boris of a huge cushion with a belt in the middle, was conspicuously silent. Thankfully, the ushers managed to separate the two families when directing them to their seats.

"Melissa's late," Danny hissed.

Boris' fleeting hopes that she had changed her mind were dashed as the Wedding March was played. Melissa entered the chapel, a vision in snow white. Despite his misgivings, he was quietly proud as he noticed the admiring glances she attracted from every male over the age of ten. Melissa's dress was breathtaking, and not just because the bill was extortionate. She wore a fitted silk sheath, accentuating every one of her curves. He realised gratefully she was wearing flat shoes so she wouldn't appear taller than him.

Boris shifted from foot to foot. While his phone was switched to silent mode, he could feel it vibrating in his pocket. He wondered anxiously about the messages he would have to field once the register was signed. At least the service was swift and smooth, with no last-minute objections from his sister. Finally, there was a ring on Melissa's finger, the obligatory kiss, signatures in front of the vicar, and he was able to plead a comfort break and respond to missives from Jed and Mark.

There was still a light frost on the ground when they emerged from the chapel, although the sun was breaking through clouds. Boris pressed the photographer to hurry with his outdoor work, pleading that Melissa would catch her death of cold otherwise. Hurrying his radiant bride to the banqueting hall, Boris told her he needed another break, and bolted for his bedroom. He poured himself a stiff whisky from the minibar, took a deep breath and rang Mark. "Do you think you could give it a rest? Send a text if it's urgent, otherwise I'll answer you tomorrow."

"Your funeral," Mark said, and Boris imagined him shrugging.

The day passed quickly, Boris graciously accepting the congratulations of his guests while drinking as much as possible. It took away the sting of his married status, and meant he laughed at Danny's rather crude speech and even another mention from Lee of dodgy stag photographs. "You mean me on my BlackBerry," he said, which raised a chuckle and a knowing glance from Melissa. Besides, he had paid for the champagne already, and might as well ensure he had value for money.

In his rare moments of reflection, he was becoming increasingly irritated with Lee. They had known each other for more than a decade. Lee, married young and supporting far too many children, had always been strapped for cash. This fact, combined with the clumsy references to Taylor's photographs and the allegedly secret car loan, convinced Boris he had identified A Wright at last. It was outrageous that a friend would behave so shabbily.

What was he to do? Tempting as it was to take Lee to one side and thump him, it would solve nothing. In spite of his inebriation, Boris was well aware that Lee was a keen amateur boxer who could knock him out with a single punch.

He had to act, though. If he could get rid of Lee, he wouldn't have to pay the latest demand from the blackmailer; in fact, he would never have to pay another penny.

"Have another glass," he urged Lee. After his success in Amsterdam, Boris was confident he could secretly increase the alcoholic content of a drink. He made sure that he took another trip to his bedroom, stuffing his pockets with vodka miniatures to slip into Lee's wineglass.

The cake, a towering confection beribboned, swagged and swirled with icing and scattered with rose petals, was cut to general acclaim.

Melissa, high on excitement and champagne, handed pieces to Lee's wife and children.

"Lee really seems unwell," Melissa said.

"Look, Diani," Boris said solicitously to Lee's wife, "Lee can stay here tonight. My room's actually free, because Melissa and I booked the honeymoon suite. You take the kids home to London now, and we'll send Lee back on the train tomorrow morning."

"That's very kind of you." She looked pale, tired and harassed. Her two youngest children, scarcely more than babies, were grizzling and clinging to her legs. Boris felt a pang of guilt about his plans for Lee, but brushed the emotion away. If Lee was capable of blackmailing one of his best buddies, what else might he do? Diani was better off without him, and anyway, Lee surely had life insurance, so she wouldn't suffer financially.

"Diani," Melissa murmured, as they watched Lee's family drive away in a newish Land Rover Defender, a car that Boris was sure he had financed. "What kind of name is that?"

"Chosen by her parents to commemorate their honeymoon destination," Boris said.

"So our first child could be called Paris?"

If we have the misfortune to start a family so quickly, Boris thought. Aloud, he said, "It could have been Bali. A lucky escape."

Melissa's orchestra chums had accompanied the hymns during the chapel ceremony. They were about to start playing waltzes and polkas. Melissa and Boris would have the first dance. "Could you ask them to wait, please?" Boris said. "I want to see how Lee's faring."

Lee was still seated at the dinner table, his head in his hands.

"Let's get you to bed," Boris suggested, tugging the man's sleeve. With difficulty, Lee rose to his feet, allowing Boris to lead him to his chamber.

"Must drink some water," Lee said.

"Here you are." Boris filled a glass with a splash from the tap and a few shots of vodka.

"Doesn't taste like water," Lee said suspiciously.

"Your tastebuds have been tainted by all that booze. Go on, it'll do you good."

"Wanna throw up," Lee said.

"You shouldn't do that," Boris said. "Lie down until you feel better." As if that was going to happen. He resisted the urge to hit the usher. However much Lee deserved it, it was too dangerous to leave evidence of a fight. Anyway, despite being plastered, Lee might best him still.

Lee staggered to the edge of the bed and slumped against it. Boris nudged, pushed and finally lifted him onto it, a dead weight. Vacantly, Lee stared at the ceiling. "The room's spinning round," he said, in a shocked tone, as if this were the most profound comment he could ever make.

"Good," said Boris, absent-mindedly. He hunted through his suitcase for ties and pairs of braces, found them, and lashed Lee's wrists and ankles to the bedposts.

"What are you doing?" Lee slurred.

"Giving nature a helping hand," Boris said. "Go to sleep, Lee." He closed the curtains and raided the minibar for more whisky miniatures, gulping the contents straight from the bottles to steady his nerves. Without looking at his erstwhile friend again, he left the room, slamming the door and hooking a 'Do Not Disturb' sign on the handle.

He danced with Melissa, glad handed his way through the rest of the party, and tipsily carried her over the threshold of the honeymoon suite at midnight.

"I'll just look in on Lee," he said, noting that Melissa had invested in Agent Provocateur white bridal underwear. "Keep that on," he called as he left the room. He rather fancied the joy of unpeeling her on his return.

He found his friend in the same position in which he had left him, vomit spilling out of his mouth and nostrils. There was no pulse, no rise and fall of the chest that would indicate Lee was still breathing. "Serves you right," muttered Boris self-righteously, alcohol having temporarily removed all capacity for guilt. Despite his lack of sobriety, he remembered to remove the ties and braces, shove them back in his suitcase, and take it with him. The hotel staff could deal with the corpse the next day, long after he and Melissa had breakfasted early on Bucks Fizz and been whisked away by taxi to catch the Eurostar to Paris.

Chapter 18 Jed talks tax

Jed's phone rang. "I want to go through the financials for Project Shield again," Mark said.

"Must we? We already paid for it."

Mark was adamant. "Yes, because we had an emergency loan from our private equity shareholders, and they want it back. We have to borrow £80m from our banks. They've insisted on a meeting with both of us tomorrow and they're expecting us to explain how we'll make money out of Project Shield. As we're relying on the tax scheme to do it, we'll need to disclose all the details. Boris and I are coming to see you now to tell you how it works."

Jed admitted defeat. There were several stress relievers on his desk, bouncy rubber balls just the right size to squeeze with his fist when he felt under pressure. Muttering under his breath, he hurled each of them at the window with as much force as he could muster. He knew the glass would not crack; it never did.

He could sense something was amiss as soon as Boris walked into the room. The tax manager's eyes were hollow, his blond hair lank and greasy. Worse, he smelled of drink. It was 10 am and Jed was less than amused. He would have sent Boris home, had Mark not impressed on him repeatedly that Boris' work was critical to GardNet's success.

Jed forced a smile. "Tell me about the tax scheme, Boris," he said. "I'll ask Val for some coffee."

"I think it's on its way," Mark said, as the door opened and Val arrived with a tray of hot drinks.

Boris drank his latte even before Jed had swallowed his espresso. Without a word, Val brought Boris another.

"OK, let's talk tax," said Boris. "I don't like to call anything a scheme, incidentally. It's structured finance."

Jed bit his lip. His dislike of Boris intensified. He did not pay his people to be pompous.

"We start by borrowing from a bank," Boris said.

"To repay our shareholders? How does that save us tax?" Jed asked.

"We don't repay the shareholders straight away. The cash goes round in a circle," Boris said. "First of all, we borrow £80m and use it to pay a dividend to the private equity investors in Luxembourg."

"You and I would normally receive dividends too, Jed, but we'll have to waive our entitlement," Mark interjected.

"I don't like the sound of that," said Jed. "Anyway, if we've used all the bank loans to pay a dividend, won't we still owe money to our shareholders?"

"Yes, but not for long," Boris said. "Our shareholders will use the cash to capitalise a Dutch company, which will transfer all of the money to a Swiss branch. Then they'll give the Dutch company to GardNet. After that, the Swiss branch will repay our shareholders."

"The accountants will book a loan from the Swiss branch to GardNet in the UK," Mark said.

"I've read about schemes like that in the Financial Times," Jed said.

"Structures," Boris muttered.

"Let me finish," Jed said sharply. "Surely this will bring us unwarranted publicity, or at the very least, an investigation by HMRC? It sounds complicated and unethical." If Eleanor were still of sound mind, she would be deeply unimpressed. He certainly wouldn't have cared to explain Boris' plans to her.

"It's not complicated at all," Boris said, draining his second cup of coffee. "GardNet will end up paying interest twice, once to the banks and once to the Swiss branch that it owns itself."

At certain moments throughout his life, Jed had experienced a sensation of straying into a parallel universe, unknown territory where nobody quite spoke the same language. That was how he felt now. A headache nagged at his temples. "That can't be legal," he muttered.

"Boris assures me it is," Mark said breezily.

"Right," Boris said. "It's totally within the law. Shall I carry on?"

"Must you?" Jed asked. Pain was spreading across his forehead and behind his eyes.

"Yes, please do, Boris," Mark said.

"We would always have had to borrow from a bank to repay our shareholders, but this way, we get a tax advantage from the Swiss branch," Boris continued. "We'll only pay 5% tax on its interest income, but we'll get tax relief at 20% on the interest paid to it from the UK." He smirked. "In fact, the larger the loan, the bigger the tax saving, so it's just as well you agreed such a high price for Project Shield."

Jed doubted it was intended as a compliment. As well as being drunk, Boris was unbearably smug. Jed pointedly ignored him and addressed his response to Mark. "When you said a tax manager would save us millions, I didn't anticipate this sort of financial engineering. Surely we don't want these shenanigans on the front page of the FT?"

"It's absolutely standard practice for private equity shareholders," Mark said. "Given the amount we paid for the call centre, they expect us to implement this structure, reputational risk or not. If you didn't want to sup with the devil, you shouldn't have taken his money to expand GardNet."

"I've set up a few other companies in the Cayman Islands and Luxembourg as well, in case we need them," Boris interjected.

"You should know what companies you need by now," Jed said. He made no effort to disguise his contempt.

Boris reddened. "I'm waiting for rulings from foreign tax authorities," he said.

"Yes, we're not keeping any secrets from them," Mark said. "It's all above board. Thanks for your work on that, Boris."

Boris was fidgeting. "I ought to return to my desk to check emails."

"You wouldn't have so many if you didn't take so much time off," Jed said.

"It was my honeymoon, Jed," Boris replied. "I spent so much of it dealing with emails that I was very nearly divorced."

"Boris," Mark said, "I'll catch up with you later, OK? I've just got some business to discuss with Jed."

"Surely not?" Jed said, only to receive a sharp kick from Mark under the glass table.

"Give the guy a break, Jed," Mark said, once Boris had left. "He's only just back from his honeymoon. He's probably exhausted."

"He's in pieces," Jed said. "Couldn't you smell the booze on his breath? He can't handle the pressure. I need managers with more stamina."

"Oh, Boris has stamina all right," Mark said, grinning wolfishly. "He really took care of a cute redhead on his stag weekend."

"What do you mean?"

"Take a look, mate." Mark jabbed at his iPhone.

"I see." Jed felt he had seen rather too much. He watched helplessly as Mark flicked through an album of photographs, all revealing more of Boris than he would wish.

"He's a legend," Mark said.

"I don't think so," Jed said icily. "Tell me, Mark, that phone of yours is company property, isn't it? And so is Boris' iPad mini, which he undoubtedly used to disseminate these filthy images. I'm calling the HR bunny now. I want him out of here."

"He didn't spread the joy," Mark said. "That was his ginger tart. She emailed the piccies to all of us. Listen, you can't fire him for that, either. I've told you how much we need Boris. If he goes, I go."

"No way." Jed was shocked by the ultimatum. He counted to ten, a technique Eleanor had often recommended, largely in vain. "All right. I accept that, without Boris, we'd lose everything. It's Hobson's choice, it seems. That scumbag can keep his job. Just don't ever make me go near him again."

He didn't see why Melissa should go near Boris again, either. She deserved better. When Mark had left his office, Jed started to play Fauré's Pavane. The flute and oboe barely soothed him as he mulled over the wisdom of a phone call to Melissa. He had her telephone number on the orchestra flyer she had given him before Christmas. If he simply told her what Boris had done, how would she take it? He didn't like bad news himself; he had noticed most people reacted irrationally to it and there was every chance Melissa was the same. She might not believe him and she might even refuse to speak to him again. No, there was a better way. Jed had administrator privileges over all GardNet computer systems, and even without them, he would have been able to hack Boris' emails in an instant. Within ten minutes, he had entered Boris' Outlook mailbox, found the email from Taylor and forwarded it from Boris to Melissa with the subject heading 'Amsterdam Pictures'.

Chapter 19 Boris hits the bottle

There were over thirty new emails waiting by the time Boris returned to his desk. One of them was from A Wright. Although it was not yet lunchtime, he put on his coat. "Grabbing some fresh air," he said to Mark, as he bumped into his boss on the way out. Mark nodded, his expression neutral. Boris rather liked his squash partner, but still bitterly regretted both inviting Mark on his stag weekend and taking the job with GardNet in the first place. He resolved to stay for a year, long enough for his CV to be enhanced by the kudos of working in a private equity environment and devising the Project Shield tax structure.

There were dozens of pubs within a quarter mile of his office. All would be relatively empty at this time of day. Boris chose a 17th century inn with free wi-fi and a vast range of single malts, ordered a double whisky and sat in the corner dealing with his emails.

First, he opened the missive from A Wright. Predictably, it was another demand for £3,000 in bitcoins. Boris recalled the indescribable shock of receiving an email from Wright on his first day in Paris. He had known then, to his horror, that he had killed one of his best friends for nothing. Even worse, the police had been in touch and it was clear they were investigating Lee's death conscientiously. Foul play hadn't been ruled out.

Wright's honeymoon email had been a reminder. Why had payment been overlooked on the wedding day, Wright asked; it surely only took moments to transfer the virtual currency, just as photographs could be emailed in the blink of an eye. Boris had taken the hint then, and did so again today. He sent Wright the bitcoins. As he had done throughout his honeymoon, Boris gulped his whisky and ordered another.

He sat in the pub for three hours, scarcely aware of the City workers popping into the hostelry for hearty lunches, concentrating only on his iPad mini and his whisky. Had Mark not phoned, he would have stayed there longer.

"Where are you, mate?"

"I went somewhere quiet to work."

"It doesn't sound quiet," Mark said, obviously hearing the murmur of well-refreshed City professionals in the background. "Listen, I know you've done some work; I've had half a dozen emails from you today.

But a three hour lunch break is out of order, mate. I want to see you back in the office."

Boris manfully downed a double whisky in one, paying the tab with his credit card. His limit hadn't been exceeded yet. He was starting to consider channelling the Project Shield funds through additional companies he had created in far flung Caribbean islands, enabling him to siphon off £60,000 or so for himself. Even better, he could take a little more and send some cash to Diani. He shuddered to think what she was going through. If he said the money had been spent on professional fees, nobody at GardNet would be any the wiser. Of course, he was aware this was fraud, but he didn't intend to break the eleventh commandment and get caught.

"What's the matter?" Mark wanted to know. "You've just married a blonde hottie. Is she so hard to satisfy that you have to spend all day getting pissed?"

"We're both shaken by what happened to Lee," Boris said. He didn't want to admit that Melissa had lost all interest in sex since hearing the news, sobbing and pushing him away when he tried to comfort her. If anything, the avalanche of emails about Project Shield were a welcome diversion from thoughts of Lee's death and the eye-watering sums he was paying Wright. For once, he wanted to be absorbed in his work.

"Yes, that was dreadful," Mark said. "I didn't realise the pressure was getting to you, mate. If you fall over, we're done for." He sounded worried. "Go home, get some rest. There's nothing that won't wait till tomorrow."

"That's not the impression I got from Jed."

Mark clapped a palm to his forehead. "Jed wants everything yesterday. He's got to learn he can't always have what he wants." He grinned. "Did I say something tactless? Listen, one piece of advice: don't let him know you've been boozing. It's too obvious. Suck cough sweets or brush your teeth before you see him. Better still, don't see him at all. Send him emails. He prefers that, anyway. Meanwhile, go home."

Boris took his advice. There was plenty of drink at his apartment, but just to make sure, he bought Scotch on his way to the DLR. He found himself sipping straight from the bottle as he travelled, oblivious to the glances of other passengers.

He did not expect Melissa to be there when he arrived. In the afternoon, she usually visited the homes of wealthy lawyers and diplomats to give their children music tuition. He was pleasantly surprised to find her flute case and handbag just inside the front door.

"Hello darling," he called cautiously, popping a cough sweet in his mouth. Jed wasn't the only individual who might look askance at the amount he drank: Melissa had, in fact, made pointed remarks during their mini-break in Paris.

He didn't hear a reply. Perhaps she was in the bathroom. Slightly concerned, he went from room to room, looking for his wife. As well as the bedroom they shared, the flat had a music room, and it was here that he found her packing a suitcase.

Her piano was festooned with a string of fairy lights. Melissa had just picked them up, and on seeing Boris, she threw them at him. The lights were followed by a coffee cup, the dregs from which spilled all over the cream carpet.

"What are you doing?" he said, rubbing the side of his head where the cup had shattered, and finding she had drawn blood.

"Don't come near me," she said. She didn't shout, and he realised she didn't have to. The quiet menace in her voice was quite unlike anything he had heard before.

"I love you Melissa," he said. "Where are you going? I don't understand."

"You've been seeing someone else," she said. "You swore to forsake all others, and you lied."

"It wasn't a lie, Melissa." To his astonishment, his lip trembled. He hadn't cried since he was a child. It must be the whisky making him maudlin.

"I've seen the photographs."

How? Why? He had paid Wright, surely? He decided to check later if the last payment had bounced for some reason, but it was scarcely relevant. Somehow, Melissa knew about Taylor. That was all that mattered.

"Look, Melissa," he said, "it's all in the past. That girl meant nothing to me. It was Mark's fault. He set me up with her on my stag weekend, for a bit of fun."

"You cared so little for me that you let your boss talk you into meaningless sex with that vixen?"

Not exactly. He had just seized an opportunity, as he had several times during their relationship. Although his lack of height seemed to deter most females, Taylor wasn't the first to succumb to his charm. He silently cursed her iPad. He had never expected Melissa to find out about any of his furtive nights of passion; had committed murder and considered fraud to prevent her from doing so. "I think the world of you, Melissa. I meant every word of my marriage vows. Please give me another chance." His voice shook.

"It's too late," Melissa said. Her tone was cold, and unlike his, devoid of tremor. "Lee's death was a bad omen, a sign that our marriage was doomed, and now I know why. I can't trust you ever again, certainly not enough to have children with you."

"Melissa, I'd be a good father," he begged, although he doubted it was true. "I'll never so much as look at another woman again."

"I don't believe you." For the first time, she betrayed a note of exasperation. "It's not as if I've never had offers. I could have had affairs with rich men. I meet so many in the course of my work. I've been pestered countless times by fathers, brothers and friends of my pupils in South Kensington and Mayfair. They gave me flowers, asked me to dinner at the Savoy, dangled holidays in Nice, Acapulco, Hong Kong. I turned them all down, every single one."

"You never brought flowers home."

"I didn't accept them." Her eyes were weary. "Leave me alone, Boris. I'll be in touch to collect the piano later, when I've found somewhere to live. Alexa from the orchestra is letting me couch surf for a few days. She'll be here at any moment to help carry my cases."

He stood in front of the suitcase. "I won't let you go."

"Then I'll have to fight you, Boris."

To his astonishment, she kneed him in the groin.

He hopped about the room in pain while she threw music books into her case. He could only have stopped her by fighting back, but he could not bear to hurt her. All he could do was watch her, admiring her blonde locks, her perfect figure, her porcelain skin; savouring the sight of her one last time before she left the flat, and his life, forever.

Chapter 20 Jed finds help

"The fragrant Melissa has walked out on young Boris," Mark told Jed.

"Oh?" This was interesting news indeed. "Then he's had his just deserts."

"Apparently, she saw some photographs," Mark said. "The same ones that you and I admired yesterday."

"She did the right thing," Jed said.

"How did she lay her hands on the photographs, I wonder? What do you think, Jed?"

"I have no idea." He rarely bothered to make eye contact with Mark, and he certainly would not do so now. Jed had been wholly truthful as a young child, until Eleanor had taught him that others might dissemble. It hadn't taken him long to see that lying could be very convenient on occasion.

Mark dropped his questions and began to babble about the accounting systems integration for Project Shield.

"You should be sorting this out yourself," Jed said. "That's why you're our chief of finance, remember?" His thoughts lay elsewhere. He remembered Jeannie, the dating coach; imagined holding her business card in his hand. Actually, he had scanned it into his smartphone. "I've got stuff to do," he said, rising from his chair and opening his office door to encourage Mark to leave.

Jeannie appeared unfazed as he stammered his request over the phone. "You want one to one coaching right now, this afternoon?" she asked. "Yes, I can reschedule my diary, but it will be expensive, I'm afraid."

She named a sum that he suspected she thought was excessive. For him, it was loose change. He agreed on the spot.

Valerie was evidently surprised when he declared he would work from home that afternoon. "You're supposed to be seeing bankers with Mark."

Jed waved dismissively. "Ask him to run the meeting solo."

"I believe they asked for you."

"I'll see them tomorrow, then."

He took a cab home, calming his nerves by working on new security software until the dating coach arrived.

Jeannie seemed impressed by his flat in St Pancras Chambers. "It has good bones," she said, scanning the arched windows and lofty ceilings.

"Why does that matter?" Jed asked, puzzled.

"You'll be inviting the lady back here, no doubt," she pointed out. "More of that later. For now, why don't you make us both a cup of coffee and tell me about her?"

Jed was proud of his coffee machine, a gleaming chrome number that hissed invitingly as he twiddled its dials. "What would you like to know?" he asked, as he prepared a latte for Jeannie. The enticing smell of fresh coffee filled his senses. He began to feel optimistic.

"Her name would be a good start."

"She's called Melissa," Jed began, "and she plays the flute."

"Who with?"

"The Orchestra of London."

"When's their next concert?"

"I don't know."

"You need to find out, because you must buy a ticket. Tell me more about Melissa."

"She was a student at the Birmingham Conservatoire."

"Anything else?"

"She is pretty. When we met, my flatmate told me she was fit."

"You met her through your flatmate?"

"At the same time. They married. But she's left him."

Jeannie looked concerned. "Jed, I'm sorry. You didn't mention she was a married lady. I'm afraid I can't help you any further. It just wouldn't be professional."

Jed felt as he had when considering a future without GardNet. All the certainties in his life, the hope of better days ahead, began to slip away from him. "She is the love of my life," he blurted. "I would treat her as she deserves. That philandering husband of hers cheated on her even before they married. She was right to walk out on him and they'll never be reconciled."

Jeannie's eyes flickered. Was she reconsidering? "Do they have children?" she asked.

"No."

"Thank goodness for that. A marriage breakdown is tough enough without them."

"A clean break is what she needs," Jed said.

"Exactly," Jeannie said. "She doesn't need a new relationship, she needs a break. She'll be feeling shocked, shattered by what's happened. If she meets someone now, on the rebound from a broken marriage, it'll never work out. She must be given time to think."

If that was what Melissa required, Jed wanted her to have it. "I agree," he said. "However long it takes, I can wait. But..."

"You want her to know you're there for her?" Jeannie said.

"Yes."

Jeannie was silent, then she said, "Actually, I think I can work with you, now I understand you, and Melissa's situation, better. Thanks for explaining it."

Jed suppressed a sigh. He was overjoyed that Jeannie was prepared to help him, and relieved he had persuaded her to his way of thinking. In his heart, he knew his influencing skills were weak. Money and status usually allowed him to call the shots, but not this time.

"Now," Jeannie said, "let's get practical. One day, you'll bring Melissa to this flat. It has to be a romantic space. Think candles, plenty of them, and a gorgeous aroma. Fresh lilies everywhere. Well done for having a tidy flat, which few gentlemen do. But your furniture doesn't match, so add some white throws."

Jed could only gawp at her. Again, he was bewildered, listening to language he did not understand. None of the other women in his life had ever spoken like this. Eleanor, he was sure, would simply have suggested he might like a few photographs around the place to make it more homely. "Run that past me again?" he said, hoping for more time to process the information.

Jeannie laughed merrily. "You look horrified. All of these things can be bought in five minutes down in the station foyer."

Jed rarely visited the shops in the station, except to buy coffee and ready meals. He allowed Jeannie to lead him through them like a whirlwind, acquiring homewares, flowers, scented soaps, chocolates and champagne. He looked askance at the last item, until Jeannie said, "You may not drink alcohol, but she does, right?"

He had never noticed so many retail outlets there. Just as the number of bags began to feel uncomfortably bulky, Jeannie said, "We should shop for you, too. Put some pizzazz into your look." A new suit, shirts, ties, cufflinks, even a leather jacket, followed swiftly.

Incredibly, all the goods were purchased and displayed in his home within two hours. He had to agree that, in some indefinable way, the flat had become classier and more spacious. The new outfits, laid on his bed, were pleasing in their cut, colour and symmetry.

He made more coffee, and Jeannie returned to her questions. "What other information can you give me? How old is she, where is she from, what does she like to do apart from playing the flute?"

"I don't know. Her musical technique is sublime."

"Jed, you and Melissa are clearly both passionate about music, which is a wonderful trait to have in common and would help you have a great life together. The more you know about her, the better your chance of winning her heart when she's ready to love again. I'm hearing loud and clear that it's her heart you want, rather than her body – am I right?"

"Yes."

"Jed, the good news is, you will have fun talking to Melissa to discover everything you don't know."

He was sceptical. "How?"

Jeannie looked straight into his eyes. "Trust me, Jed. Here's our strategy. First, you will go to her next concert."

Chapter 21 Boris moves on

Boris compensated for Melissa's departure in the only way he could: by drinking more whisky. He began to average a bottle a day, starting with a snifter before breakfast and then drinking from a hip flask at his desk. Mark said nothing to him about it, although he clearly knew what Boris was doing. Boris continued to deal efficiently with his emails, directing lawyers in far flung jurisdictions to set up companies there. A handful of messages arrived from A Wright. At first, Boris ignored them. Eventually, he sent Wright a terse reply, saying he had called the police. Naturally, he had not done so and would not. There was no point drawing attention to a possible motive for despatching Lee, whose death, to Boris' relief, finally appeared to have been treated as a sad accident. Nevertheless, the threat was enough to silence the blackmailer.

He was still suspicious of Szymon. The Pole annoyed him, referring to the heaviness of his shopping bags as bottles clinked together within them, and asking with a smirk when Mrs Brooks would be back.

"She's visiting friends," Boris told him. He assumed Melissa was still at Alexa's tiny flat in Streatham. He had no means of contacting his wife. She didn't reply to calls and emails, and had unfriended him on Facebook.

He didn't know who had dropped the grenade that ended his marriage. Whether it was Szymon or not, the Pole's insolence deserved to be punished. Boris decided that a brief email to the apartment block's managers wouldn't go amiss. He stopped short of accusing Szymon of any crimes outright, merely claiming that parcels had gone astray when Szymon was manning the reception desk.

A reply told him that the management company regarded his allegations as serious, and they would be investigated promptly. He did not see Szymon again. When he casually asked a receptionist where the Pole had gone, the man shrugged and said he supposed Szymon was working at another block nearby.

Evenings were becoming lighter. Having steeled himself to spend them hunting houses and choosing furniture with Melissa, Boris struggled to fill the unexpected gap with work and whisky. He found succour in the companionship of those of his friends who remained stubbornly single.

"Coming clubbing on Saturday?" Danny asked. "Beats drinking yourself into a stupor."

As ever, the pair looked extraordinarily ill-matched, with Danny towering above his friend. They paid a substantial ticket price and even more for champagne, with Boris happily dipping into his pocket now the burden of bankrolling Wright had been lifted.

Danny nudged him. "See those girls over there? Let's send them some champagne."

Boris drew a finger across his throat. "The last time I did that, it ended badly."

"Only one way to get over Melissa. Find someone new."

"I haven't given up on her, Danny. I need to see her. I'm going to her next concert."

"At least hedge your bets," Danny said. "Just tell me why you came to this meat market if you weren't hoping to pull."

Boris acquiesced. "Make it pink champagne," he suggested. Covertly, he studied the girls, two buxom brunettes in skimpy dresses. He mentally rehearsed chat-up lines.

"This is Caz," Danny said. "Please excuse us, Boris. Penelope and I want to dance."

Boris prepared to be charming. "What brings you here?" he asked.

"I want to extend my social circle," she said, flashing an attractive smile. "I've just left a long-term relationship and I want to get out more."

"Me too," Boris said. "What a coincidence." He expected 95% of the clubbers were hoping to meet new people, although it was debatable whether they would stay in touch for more than 24 hours.

"Did you know you look extraordinarily like Boris Johnson?"

"It has been mentioned."

"But you're not."

"I'm no politician, merely a humble finance manager." Boris was enough of a diplomat to refrain from saying that his job was to save GardNet as much tax as possible.

"I'm a teacher," Caz said. "In London, but I want to move to Kenya."

"Where – Diani?" Apart from the capital, it was the only town in Kenya that Boris could name.

"That's a beach resort, isn't it? No, I'm going to a small village on the shores of Lake Victoria. I want to set up a school there, and I'm raising funds at the moment. It's why my boyfriend and I split, actually. He wanted me to stay here and start a family, and that's the last thing I'm going to do."

This was music to Boris' ears. He determined at once to take Caz home that night.

Chapter 22 Jed makes a move

The Orchestra of London was playing Mozart concertos at a suburban hall in Richmond. Jed took a cab from his office. He was wearing his new leather jacket and a blue checked shirt that Jeannie said brought out the colour of his eyes. "Keep it light," he muttered to himself. "Keep it fun."

Like many second-rate venues, there was no allocated seating. Arriving in good time, Jed sat near the front and studied the programme. There would be a few short pieces, then Mozart's Concerto for Flute, Harp and Orchestra in C Major. Jed knew this was regarded by Mozart fans as rather a curiosity, and awaited it with anticipation. He was not disappointed. After a lively introduction, Melissa gracefully began to play her part in tandem with the harpist, a sulky-looking youth. Jed watched avidly, drinking in her presence, overwhelmed by the joy of the piece as the notes bubbled around him.

"Bravo." When the orchestra finished, he rose straight to his feet, clapping hard.

The musicians bowed and smiled. As they left the stage, he noticed Boris Brooks for the first time that evening. The tax manager was sidling around the stage, a bunch of white flowers in his fist.

Brooks had spoiled every meeting Jed had ever had with Melissa. Would he do so again? Jed followed the orchestra and Brooks backstage, determined that this time he would win. He found Brooks arguing with a large fair-haired woman, whom he recognised as the lead violin. With her firm stance and argumentative expression, she reminded him of nothing so much as a Valkyrie.

"She doesn't want to see you," the woman was saying, barring Brooks' way.

"Can I help?" Jed asked. "I'm a friend of Melissa's."

"No, you're not," Brooks spat, seeming to forget that Jed could have him clearing his desk's contents into a bin liner with a mere snap of his fingers.

The violinist ignored him. She turned appealing blue eyes to Jed. "We need to get Melissa home, away from this bastard."

"Leave it to me," Jed said. "I have a taxi waiting outside."

He squeezed past her, while the Valkyrie continued to block Brooks.

Melissa's flute was in its case, and she was buttoning a coat over her sparkly evening gown.

"You need to leave now," Jed said. "I have a cab outside for you."

She eyed him suspiciously. "I haven't ordered one. I can't afford taxis."

"I'm paying," Jed said. "I'm Jed Gardner. Don't you remember? I've always been a fan."

To his dismay, Melissa shrank from him. "Of course. I recognise you now. My ex's boss and former flatmate. I suppose you're here with him."

"No." Jed had not anticipated this reaction. He searched his vocabulary for a response that would build her trust. "You gave me a flyer for the orchestra, remember?" he faltered, afraid of sounding lame. "Purely by chance, I decided to come along tonight and when I saw you were having some bother with Boris, I thought I'd help." He added, "Your first violin can't fend off Boris forever, so please hurry. My taxi's waiting."

Melissa smiled, probably with relief. "Lead on," she said, following him out of the green room door and into the night. Jed was thankful that Val had booked the cab for the whole evening, telling the driver to wait throughout the performance.

"Streatham," Melissa told the driver.

"Then St Pancras," Jed added.

"That'll take a while." The cabbie was dubious.

"Not a problem," Jed said. He turned to Melissa, helping with her seatbelt. "Your performance was magnificent."

"Thank you. I think my colleagues played well too," Melissa said loyally, appearing to give no thought to the fact that Jed had travelled from north London to Surrey in order to see a little known orchestra. "Actually, do you think we could take Alexa home as well? She's the first violin."

"You may well see Mr Brooks again, too, if we wait for her," Jed warned.

Melissa shivered. "You're right. Let's go now." She made the decision just in time, for her words were followed by banging on the window next to her. Brooks had broken free of the Valkyrie, and was shouting at them, words that were buried in the roar of the engine as the driver revved away from him.

They would be together for about thirty minutes, Jed thought, and this was his chance. Suddenly tongue-tied, he struggled to find a topic of conversation.

Melissa came to the rescue. "I know you enjoyed our performance, because you gave us a standing ovation. You can't imagine what it means to us to be appreciated so much."

"You deserved it," Jed said. "Mozart is probably my favourite composer too. At least, he's up there in my top ten."

"And mine," Melissa said. "I love the sheer exuberance of his work." Jed nodded.

"What do you play?" she asked.

"I just listen." Jed blushed. It was a matter of some regret that his co-ordination had always been too poor to play an instrument well. Despite finding a computer keyboard easy to use, Eleanor's piano had defeated him.

He finally remembered Jeannie's advice: ask her all about herself, and keep it light. "What was your first instrument?" he asked.

"The recorder." She laughed. "I have fond memories of primary school concerts in Brighton. I soon graduated to the flute, though, and it's been my life ever since."

Jed wondered whether to admit how much music, and in particular Melissa's interpretation of the classics, could move him. He chose instead to ask a question that had been puzzling him since they first met. "How does Boris fit into that? I mean, I've shared a flat with him and worked with him, and never seen any evidence that he appreciates Mozart or any other composer."

She looked confused. "He came to the concert this evening."

"Because you were there."

"Oh, I see." Melissa was momentarily silent; lost in thought, perhaps. Finally, she said, "I suppose then, like my family, my ex wasn't musical but just wanted to give me support. He went to a lot of concerts." She bit her lip. "I thought I knew him and now I don't think I ever really did. Jed?"

"Yes?" he asked, thrilled to hear her voice saying his name.

"Please can we not talk about my ex?"

What else could he say? Jed recalled Jeannie saying that London's villages were worth mentioning. Citizens would wax lyrical for hours about their favourite spots. "How do you like Streatham?" he asked.

"It's a place to live, that's all. I preferred Greenwich. There was more to do there; walks by the river, bars, plenty of space in the flat I shared with my ex. But I had to move out, and Alexa offered me a couch in her bedsit."

"Not even a room of your own?"

"No, and Alexa snores."

"You should move."

"My only other option is returning to my parents in Brighton. I can't afford my own place in London. The Orchestra barely breaks even. Other than that, I earn tutorial income from teaching tone-deaf kids in Kensington. It's not enough. I should have tried harder to be financially independent. I concentrated on music, not money, and here I am."

"You could stay with me," he ventured. "I have a spare room." It contained a huge model train set, though. Jed girded himself to make the ultimate sacrifice for Melissa, and pack it away. After all, he could still stroll to the platforms of St Pancras and admire real trains when the fancy took him. He remembered travelling on trains with one or two other boys from his school as a sixth former, writing down details of the engines they saw. Occasionally chancing upon adult spotters, they found themselves accepted as useful members of the team. Enjoying the camaraderie, it was the first time he had realised he could make a contribution in the adult world and be appreciated for it.

He shook the memories away. Melissa had not answered him. "I live centrally, and I'm told my flat has a good acoustic," he said.

"Thanks. I'll consider it."

There was no particular enthusiasm there, he thought. She hadn't even expressed a desire to see the room. The taxi was crossing Clapham Common now, and would soon reach Streatham. Jed desperately wanted to see Melissa again. "I'd like to take you to dinner," he suggested. "When will you be free?"

To his relief, she agreed, and he had another meeting with Jeannie to plan the dinner. He would book a table at the Gilbert Scott restaurant at St Pancras, they decided. He should offer Melissa cocktails and champagne, even if he abstained himself. The restaurant was impressive, of course, but what really counted was its location, almost directly below Jed's apartment.

The dinner was more convivial than any Jed had experienced in his life. Women like to laugh, Jeannie had told him, and Jed had looked up some jokes online and made an effort to memorise them. Seeing Melissa enjoying herself, he felt less awkward than he had expected.

He paid the bill and suggested they walk to the taxi rank. "Unless you'd like to stay?" he asked. "I live in St Pancras Chambers, just above here."

It was as if he had pressed a switch, and the light in her eyes had flickered out. "You couldn't wait, could you? It's all about sex, for you guys, isn't it?" she said, her tone frosty.

He flushed. "You should know me better than that," he said quietly. "When have you heard the slightest rumour that it's all about sex for me?" He marvelled at how quickly the words had come to his mind, and to his lips without a hint of a stammer.

It was her turn to redden. "I'm sorry," she said. "I never heard anything to that effect about my ex either – until I discovered he'd used his stag party to cheat on me."

"Perhaps he drank too much and made a bad decision," Jed said. He suspected that was the case anyway, and he could afford to be generous about Boris Brooks now. Melissa had moved out of the flat in Greenwich, and it seemed she could not even bear to say Brooks' name. He continued, "You know, I just want to make sure you're happy. I've offered my spare room to you, and I mean it. I'm not expecting anything more than a flatmate. Please go back to Streatham if that's what you want. I'll always be there for you, though, and I'd like to see you again."

He must have said the right thing. She smiled, and gently kissed him on the cheek.

Chapter 23 Szymon's homecoming

Szymon knew who to blame. "It's that asshole in the penthouse," he said, his ruddy complexion flushing even more as he drank Piotr's homebrew.

"Never mind, friend." Piotr was sympathetic. "I'll fix you up with some work. My boss can always use another labourer on the site."

"What's the pay like?"

Piotr scratched his head. "That I don't know. As an electrician, I make about ten pounds an hour. For a labourer, though, it'll be less."

Szymon sighed. "They always underpay us, those Brits, and treat us like dirt. They told me that concierge job would lead to a better position, arranging travel for the stars, walking the Queen's dogs. What happens? They only wanted a big strong security guard. They lied to me, just like that asshole lied to them. Now it's back to the building sites, outside in all weathers, snow, ice, rain. Maybe a job one day, no job the next. What's my wife going to say?"

"She'll be sympathetic, no doubt," Piotr said.

"You haven't met her," Szymon said, gloomily.

The wind was blowing from the east when he returned to Beckton. The air stank of shit: a sweet, cloying stench that made Szymon gag. Here, there were none of the cafe bars and boutiques of Greenwich, just row upon row of cheap housing, downmarket retail parks, and, of course, the shit. All of London's shit came here.

Szymon staggered to the barrack-like apartment block where he lived with Marta and Tomasz, in a two bedroom flat overlooking a car park. Any sort of vehicle was beyond their means, but little Tomasz liked to amuse himself counting the cars and announcing the different colours. Szymon was proud of the boy. The child was bright. Perhaps one day he would be a doctor, or a lawyer, living in Greenwich or better still, the old quarter of Warsaw.

Marta was waiting for him. "What time do you call this?" she wanted to know. "I'm serving breakfast at the club tomorrow. We both need to be up early, as you'll have to get Tomasz to school." She sniffed suspiciously at the air around his face.

"I needed a drink," Szymon said, in an injured tone. "I lost my job, thanks to that nasty, lying asshole I told you about."

"You did what? Then how are we going to pay the rent on this dump?"

"Piotr will find me something else. On a building site."

"You've been with that good-for-nothing drunk? No wonder you're in such a state. Nobody will employ you if you turn up smelling like that. You should have been more careful. There aren't jobs here for the taking any more."

Szymon's anger, briefly suppressed by alcohol, returned. It was hardly his fault they were in this predicament. "Shit can happen to anybody," he retorted.

"You're not just anybody, you're my husband. Just my luck to be married to a waster and a drunkard."

That was too much to bear. He shoved her to one side. "I'm going to bed. Leave me alone."

Marta reeled, gripping the side of the sofa to catch her balance. She grabbed his arm. "No you don't. We need to talk." She was shouting.

"What is there to say?" Szymon kept his voice low. He didn't want Tomasz to wake, to see them like this. He shook his arm, trying to dislodge her, but still she clung to it. He slapped her face.

The shock broke Marta's hold, but she wasn't finished. She picked up a book, one with a hard cover, and brought it down on his head with more force than he would have imagined possible. The spine broke and pages fluttered out. It had been one of the boy's school texts. Bright pictures of zoo animals lay strewn on the light wood floor.

He was still grappling with her when he heard the child's voice. "Mum, Dad, what are you doing?"

"Play-acting," he said, desperately hoping his son would believe him. "Go to sleep."

Chapter 24 Jed's flatmate

Jed was immersed in monthly sales figures when Valerie interrupted his meeting to say Melissa was on the line.

"Raj, Mark, I need to take this call alone," he said. He was accustomed to ordering them to leave his office when it suited him. By the speed with which they obeyed, they were obviously used to it too.

Melissa had good news. "Jed, you offered me a room at your place, rent-free until..."

He interrupted. "Rent-free for as long as you like."

"When can I move in?"

She and Alexa hadn't exactly quarrelled, it transpired. Both kept their small room tidy, they took turns to cook, and even the snoring was tolerable. They had realised that both wanted to practice at the same time of day, however.

"Musical differences," Jed said. He meant it in all seriousness, and was surprised when Melissa laughed.

"We might say that if we left the orchestra," she explained. "Luckily, the Orchestra of London is still very much my passion. And Alexa's."

Jed's heart sang. In future, he might be included in Melissa's passions. That day seemed to be drawing nearer. He imagined candles lighting a dark evening, and Melissa playing the flute to lighten his spirits. She had mentioned a piano too. The highlight of many childhood days had been Eleanor's renditions of Beethoven piano pieces. He had always particularly enjoyed the dulcet tones of Für Elise. He played it now, to remember old times, before he asked Valerie to reconvene the meeting.

"Did I hear you singing, Jed?" Mark asked.

"I may have hummed a tune badly." Jed blushed. "Melissa is moving into my flat."

"What, Melissa Brooks?"

"Stevens. She's getting a divorce."

"Whatever." Mark whistled. "You didn't lose any time getting in there, mate."

"Our relationship is platonic."

"Pull the other one! Who's going to believe that?"

"Can we revisit the sales figures, please?" Raj interjected.

To Valerie's evident surprise, Jed left the office early, taking a cab as usual to avoid the crowds on the street and in the Tube. As his habit was to leave long after the rush hour, he found the slowly oozing streams of traffic an annoyance. He distracted himself by playing Sudoku on his smartphone and listening to more classical music.

He had barely time to heat a ready meal and light candles before Melissa arrived. The train set didn't need to be put in boxes at all; instead, he had managed to fit it into his own bedroom, where it curved in what he thought was an elegant U shape around his bed.

"Welcome to my humble abode," he said, another prepared phrase. He took his cue from their recent parting and kissed her cheek.

"Thank you. That smells delicious, by the way." She took a deep breath, with evident pleasure.

"I hoped you might play the flute afterwards, when you'd unpacked."

"I'd love to. Any requests?"

There were so many pieces he could choose. "Let me think."

Melissa laughed. "I can't promise to be a classical jukebox for you."

"Melissa, you decide. All I ask is that you treat me to Für Elise when your piano's here."

Chapter 25 Lianne reads the news

"My treat," Caz said, "because we're networking."

"We are?" Lianne raised an eyebrow. "I thought we were a couple of schoolfriends catching up over coffee."

"I'd like an introduction to your ex-boyfriend, Andrew."

"I didn't realise you carried a torch for him," Lianne said, slightly shocked. "I can't see that he's your type. I mean, unless you book an appointment to have dinner with him a month in advance, you'll never see him."

"I want his money rather than his love."

"Interesting," Lianne said. Had she viewed their relationship in those terms, perhaps she and Andrew would still be an item.

Caz laughed. "I've made up my mind. I'm definitely moving to Kenya to set up a school there. Andrew's the CEO of a big company, isn't he? I really hope he'll give a donation to the project. Even if he won't dip into his own pocket, perhaps his company will. These large corporations all give megabucks to charity. It makes them look good, even though they might be paying their staff peanuts and avoiding all their tax."

"In that case, by introducing you, I'd be doing you both a favour."

"Exactly," Caz said. "Anyway, I've got a new boyfriend."

"I'm all ears." Lianne was enjoying herself so much, she had forgotten to order any cake.

"Yes, Penelope found him for me at a club. He's called Jonathan. You know what? He looks spookily like Boris Johnson."

"No way!" A niggling concern was beginning to bother Lianne. "Surely not Jonathan Brooks?"

"Yes…Why?"

In response, Lianne rather sorrowfully extracted a newspaper from her capacious handbag. "He features in this morning's rag." Mere chance had drawn her eyes to the story when she was idly glancing at her neighbour's newspaper on the Tube. Other people's books and papers, she always found, were far more intriguing than her own. Her curiosity awoken – she had, after all, heard about the dramatis personae from Mark and Andrew – she had taken her own copy of the freesheet to read while she waited for Caz.

"No!" Caz said, scanning the article. "The GardNet Triangle is the hottest gossip among geeks this morning. GardNet famously commands its staff to show Passion, Power and Purpose. We think head geek Jed Gardner has done just that in stealing newly-wed Melissa from tax guru Jonathan Brooks. Jilted Jonathan says, 'I still love my wife and want her back.' Millionaire Jed says, 'No comment,' but a close friend confides, 'Jed is smitten. He was the world's worst workaholic, but now he leaves his office early every day.'"

"Tells you all you need to know," Lianne said. To cheer Caz up, she added, "The chocolate cake here is superb and it's more reliable than any man. Let's grab a slab. Then you can tell me how much money you want from Andrew's company, and we'll work out how to get it."

Chapter 26 Boris makes plans

Boris took a free newspaper from the stack on display at the DLR station. Flicking through the pages, it didn't take him long to notice his starring role in the business section. He sipped nervously from his hip flask, dismayed that his misery was now public. He was also puzzled at the comments attributed to him. While they were broadly true, he didn't remember speaking to the press. Had he been so drunk that he'd given an interview without any recollection of it?

Mark was already in meetings when Boris arrived at work. Until he could see his boss, the tax manager devoted his time to emails, hoping Jed wouldn't walk past. If he saw the man who had cuckolded him, he knew rage would grip him. He could ill afford a fist fight; it would mean losing his job at a time when he was overloaded with debt.

Despite copious quantities of whisky, Boris' mood didn't improve. He received two text messages: one from Marianne, saying she had always known Melissa was a gold-digging bitch, and another from Caz, dumping him. She was surprised to learn he was married and not as free to start a new relationship as he'd suggested, she didn't need such complications in her life, and therefore, they should no longer see each other.

Mark finally surfaced a few minutes before noon, when Boris was just about to leave for the pub.

"How are you doing, mate?"

"I'd feel better without all the fuss over the GardNet Triangle."

Mark rolled his eyes. "Wouldn't we all? Even Jed thinks it's a load of HR shit. What are you worrying for, anyway? You'll get your bonus." He tapped the side of his nose. "Uncle Mark will see you all right."

The promised bonus was all that stood between Boris and a resignation letter. He was still up to his neck in debt as a result of his wedding, a ceremony that had turned out to be totally pointless. Instead of securing his future with Melissa, it had at least indirectly led to him losing her. He sighed. "Have you seen a newspaper this morning?"

"No. Red-eye taxi from Chelsea this morning, straight into meetings with Jed at 6 am. Why?"

"The GardNet Triangle has another connotation altogether." Boris noticed Mark looking away for a fraction of a second as the penny dropped, and added, "You weren't aware of any press interest, were you?"

"I did have a drink with a journalist mate a couple of days ago," Mark admitted. "I told him you were devastated by developments in your personal life."

"Anything else?" Boris asked, the seed of suspicion growing into a flourishing tree of doubt. "For example, that I hoped my wife would come back?"

"I might have said that," Mark said. "What's your problem? You do, don't you?"

"My girlfriend was less than impressed."

Mark ostentatiously bashed his forehead against the thin plasterboard that served as an office wall. "Blimey, mate, you don't hang about. Bed still warm from the wife and you've persuaded another woman in there. Don't let Jed find out; he'll be furious."

"Jed, furious with me?" Boris could not believe the irony. "He steals my wife, it's splashed all over the media, and he has the gall to be annoyed with me? I tell you, Mark, if I see him again, I'm going to knock his lights out."

"Ha ha, of course you wouldn't," Mark said hurriedly, showing by his demeanour that he expected Boris to do exactly that.

"That, or walk out." The bonus could go down the toilet for all he cared now. He would find a well-paid position elsewhere, or more likely, sell his flat and take a break to intensify his acquaintance with the whisky bottle; anything to escape from Jed Gardner and the guilt, pain and shame of having lost a friend, money and his wife in quick succession.

"You don't need to do that either," Mark said. "How are you getting on negotiating tax rulings? Do we actually need employees in any of these fiscally forgiving foreign countries?"

"Only in Zug."

"Where?"

"Switzerland. Zug is a low-tax region near Zurich. Lots of multinationals have offices there. They're happy to find room for another one as long as we employ somebody to operate it."

"I have an idea," Mark said. "You could move to Zug and run the branch for us. In fact, you could move straight away if you prefer. You don't have to be sitting in this office to implement the structure. Half the time, you're in the pub, anyway."

Mark had noticed, then. "I want a pay rise," Boris said. "Zug is crowded with multinational companies saving tax. The cost of living is stratospheric." He wasn't sure whether this was actually the case, but with luck, neither Mark nor that pretty HR manager, Lucy, would check.

"Of course," Mark said.

"And a rent allowance," Boris said. He would let out the Greenwich property, but he hardly needed to mention that to Mark. He congratulated himself on his negotiating skills. They should have sent him to the meeting with Andrew Aycliffe. Unlike Jed Gardner, he wouldn't have been hoodwinked into agreeing an outrageously stupid price for that call centre. It did mean more money in the tax structure, though. Boris decided he deserved to help himself to some of it in recompense for his troubles.

Chapter 27 Szymon and the law

"Get up and clean your shit." Anna was hammering on the door of his room. Bleary eyed, Szymon switched on the light, pulled on a jumper and yanked at the handle. With a creak, the door opened. He made a mental note to check the hinges.

His room was the smallest in the house, an extra bedroom to add to the five official ones. While mostly the house's fixtures were of good quality, his cubbyhole had been jerry-built by sectioning off part of the top landing with plywood. To compensate for his cramped quarters, he paid less rent than anyone else.

"It's Saturday morning. Why do I need to get up?" he asked Anna, speaking Polish like her.

"You left our kitchen in a state last night," she grumbled. "I spend all day, all week, cleaning at work. I'm not cleaning up after you too."

She was a good-looking girl, in her twenties, with an enviable figure. Still he would not have liked to be Andrzej, her boyfriend. Sharing a room with her, there would be no escape from her bossiness. She was trouble, 24-7.

Anna looked around his windowless box, at the narrow mattress, open suitcase with neatly folded clothes, and the piece of rickety furniture their landlord had euphemistically called a computer desk. This was where he kept the equipment Piotr had shown him how to use: glass jars and pipes full of amber liquid. "It reeks like a brewery in here," she sniffed.

In Szymon's opinion, his room smelled better than the rest of Beckton. "I'm making beer."

"Drinking it too," she snapped. "Come on, when are you getting up?"

Ravi, the young Indian student, was in the kitchen, making toast. "Want some?" he asked, his mouth full of crumbs.

"If it doesn't make too much mess."

Ravi chuckled. "That's what the shouting was about, then. Anna's a good sort you know. She makes sure the house is tidy for all of us."

"She doesn't do anything herself. I've seen Andrzej cooking for the pair of them."

"And why shouldn't he? They both work. Anyway, that's what women want these days. I'd rather have a wife with a good job, a doctor or an accountant perhaps, than someone who does all the domestic chores for me."

"Don't you people have servants back home?"

Ravi shrugged. "Sure we do. I may not return to India when I've finished my degree, though. There are more opportunities here, or in North America. The world's my oyster. Isn't that what brings you here too – to seek success and adventure?"

Szymon yawned and stretched, then sat at the table with his housemate. There were a mere four chairs in the kitchen; this in a house occupied permanently by ten people, and occasionally by any number of overnight guests. After a week on the building site, he ached all over: arms, legs, back. He would be forty in a few months and should not be labouring any longer. It was a young man's game. "It was my intention to progress," he said. "I found work quickly when I first came here. I was a concierge in an apartment block. I was assured there would be promotion to a better position, but it didn't happen. Worse, I was accused of theft, and fired, although I stole nothing."

"Oh? How long did you work there?" Ravi looked intensely interested.

"Four years."

"Did they go through disciplinary procedures, perhaps, and give you a golden handshake?"

"Did they hell." Szymon's indignation bubbled to the surface. "No. After all those years, long hours, inconvenient shifts, poor pay, there was nothing. No money, no notice, no respect, no talking about it. They chose to believe a liar's word against mine, and I was out. My wife took our son back to Poland, I couldn't pay the rent on our flat, and I ended up here." He had heard talk of the Black Hole of Calcutta, and prudently decided not to mention it. "Here I am, living in a cupboard and working in a rough job, below my capabilities. It wasn't worth coming to London, and it's hardly worth staying."

"I suppose during your four years as a concierge, they were paying you the minimum wage?"

"You must be joking. I don't earn that now and I didn't earn it then."

"Interesting," said Ravi, softly. "I'm training to be a lawyer, you know, and I bet I can get some money from that apartment company for you."

"How?"

"They were breaking the law. You should have received the legal minimum wage. Not only that, but you must have been on at least a week's notice, and they should have paid you for it. And, if they didn't properly investigate the charges against you, you have a claim for unfair dismissal."

"What does that mean?"

"About £2,000. I'll make a claim for you if you give me 20% when the company pays you. No win, no fee, eh?" He slapped Szymon's back.

Szymon did not respond. £2,000 was a fortune. What could he do with it? It would be the deposit on another flat, if he could persuade Marta to return.

"All right, 10%," Ravi said, mistaking Szymon's silence for disquiet about the size of his cut.

"It's a deal."

"That's settled then," Ravi said brightly. "And don't you worry, I'll squeeze that cash out of them quickly. They were foolish not to pay you the minimum wage. "

"Why?" Szymon asked, curious. "Isn't it good business practice?"

"It's against the law. HM Revenue & Customs administers compliance with the national minimum wage, and they're responsible for taxes as well. That means I can threaten to report the apartment company to HMRC if they don't pay up. Nobody wants the taxman on their tail."

"Let me make you a cup of tea, Ravi." Considerably cheered, Szymon set about cleaning the kitchen.

Chapter 28 Jed's joy

"I told Val not to put any calls through to me," Jed complained.

He could imagine Mark grinning. "She knows you'll make an exception for your old mate, Mark," GardNet's CFO said.

"What do you want?" Jed asked, with bad grace.

"I'm worried about Boris. He's on the edge of a nervous breakdown."

"Hardly my affair."

"Oh, I think it is," Mark said, "on every level. And I think we can help him by treating him kindly and..."

"Stop right there," Jed said. Mark was becoming too emotional. Perhaps he was spending too much time with Lucy from HR; he was beginning to sound like her. "Why should we give him special treatment? I'm going to tell Brooks to man up." He slammed the phone down. "Val!" he yelled, loud enough to summon his startled PA from her antechamber. "Get Boris Brooks for me."

"You want him to come here?"

"On the phone. Please." He had no desire to see the man's face.

It seemed to take an inordinate length of time, but finally, she called to tell him Brooks was on the line.

"Why isn't my tax scheme ready yet?" Jed barked. "If it's supposed to save money, then I'm losing cash every day you can't be bothered to finish it."

To his credit, Brooks did not mention the word 'structure'. After a long silence, he muttered something about moving to Switzerland, apparently at Mark's request.

Jed was overjoyed. With Brooks in Switzerland, Melissa was even less likely to change her mind and return to him. "Get over there as quickly as possible," he commanded. Ending the call abruptly, he ordered Val to help Brooks book flights and accommodation.

Next, he phoned Mark. "Why didn't you tell me you were moving that little squirt to Zug? It's a stroke of genius."

"I was about to let on when you hung up," Mark said. The relief in his voice was palpable, even to Jed.

Again, Jed left the office early. His flat now felt more homely, and not just because Melissa was physically present. Her existence manifested itself in other ways too. She had filled each room with fresh flowers and she liked to cook: healthy soups and stews of the sort that had bubbled away in Eleanor's kitchen nearly twenty years before. He had never been happier in his adult life. Soon he hoped, with Jeannie's help, to persuade Melissa to become more than a flatmate.

There was a Mozart symphony playing and an appetising aroma wafting through the flat when he returned to St Pancras Chambers.

"I've been to the market," Melissa announced. "We'll have parsnip soup and home-made bread, and then I must dash. At the very last minute, Alexa and I were asked to play at a charity ball in South Ken."

"South Kensington?" Jed pictured the rush hour-clogged roads from which he had just escaped. "The traffic's dreadful. You'll have to leave right away."

"I'll travel on the Tube." Melissa rolled her eyes. In spite of that, he knew she could not be exasperated, because she then said, "Would you like to go as well? I'm sure the organisers would find a place for you, especially as I'm doing them a favour."

"I've brought work home," he said. While this was true, it was not the whole story. An evening glad handing strangers was too stressful to contemplate. Jed had no illusions. He would not be left alone, whatever his demeanour. His wealth, and the recent, unwelcome newspaper stories, would ensure he received far too much attention.

Chapter 29 Andrew's evening

Andrew had arranged to meet Lianne at a bar on Kensington High Street. Smart in a white tuxedo, he was not in the least self-conscious as he waited for her. It was the sort of area, he imagined, where it was common to see men wearing dinner jackets in the early evening. Still, he looked at his Rolex. She was late.

Finally, she breezed through the door, stunning in a fur jacket and sapphire-blue evening gown that exactly matched her eyes. Andrew noticed that all the men in the room turned to look at her. She was pretty enough, but what really made her stand out was her poise. Lianne's posture was confident, tall and unshakable, despite her improbably high stiletto heels.

"Is there time for a drink?" she asked.

"I don't think so. We're expected at the Orangery." He looked meaningfully at her shoes. "Shall I call a cab?"

"No," Lianne laughed. "I can walk." Still graceful, she easily matched his stride as they strolled through Kensington Gardens. Houses even larger than Andrew's Midlands mansion rose to the left of them, many in the wedding cake stucco style popular in the more monied parts of London: huge diplomatic residences, or the homes of foreign billionaires.

The Orangery, a handsome redbrick pavilion, was glowing in the last of the evening sun. While a black-clad waiter was serving fizz to the smokers who stood outside puffing in the chilly air, Andrew decided it was too cold to linger. He ushered Lianne inside, to be greeted with glasses of champagne: an expensive marque, he observed.

Lianne noticed too. "How will the Kidsworld charity make money when it throws Moët at all the guests?"

Andrew grinned. "I think you can work it out – especially once I tell you each ticket cost £300. If that wasn't enough, be assured there are some folk here tonight with deep pockets. They'll be expected to pledge large sums to Kidsworld later on."

She scanned the room, evidently curious. "I don't recognise anyone."

"They may not be celebs, but they've got money. Serious money. Lady Anne Barrett over there owns half a merchant bank. She's talking to Hugh Penfielding, who runs a FTSE100 company."

"So even if they don't open their own wallets, their companies will give large donations. To make them look good in public," Lianne said thoughtfully.

"Exactly."

"How about you?"

"Kidsworld is Madrigal's charity of the year, so I'll be handing over a cheque for twenty grand later."

"I don't suppose," Lianne said, her eyes flashing, "that you could also spare some cash to build a school in Kenya? A little money goes a long way there. You could really make a difference to an old friend of mine, who's raising funds to help orphans. There will be a new school, a farm to support the children and a basic medical centre. Somewhere to get vaccinations, clean water, first aid and other services we take for granted in London."

"And take for granted in Birmingham, even," he gently reminded her. "Yes, I'm sure I can help. How much does he need?"

"She." Lianne stopped, and looked at him sharply. "There was a twinkle in your eye when I said that, Andrew. Are you not dating at the moment?"

"No time," Andrew admitted. "I'm working and playing too hard. My mother despairs of me." Rightly, he thought. Most men would have a partner at his age, if not a family. He was convinced she thought he was gay, which was far from true. "How about you? Women are supposed to feel broody as they hit thirty – is it happening?"

"I'm not there yet, and I don't need a baby or a man," Lianne said, in tones that suggested she didn't want them either. "I've got other plans. Once I've completed on my flat, I'll let it and go travelling. I might even join Caz in Kenya."

"What about your coaching clients?"

"They'll manage." She shrugged. "You asked earlier how much Caz needed. She'll take as much or as little as you can spare, Andrew. I'd think anyone running a large company, living in a mansion and driving a sports car could spare a few thousand pounds."

"Of course," he agreed, marvelling at her adroit change of subject. "Ask her to email me." He added, just in case there was the slightest chance, "We could give it a try again, Lianne. You're right; I have a superb lifestyle. Some would say I'd make a great husband and father."

"I wouldn't say so," Lianne retorted. "You have the money, but not the time."

He felt he had pushed her enough. Lianne was already doing him a favour by escorting him to the ball. Other captains of industry were now hailing him, and she cheerfully made conversation with them, graciously accepting champagne and making it clear she and Andrew were just friends.

The dinner was a good networking opportunity for him. Several guests expressed an interest in Madrigal's software. This, in truth, was why he attended such events. Of course, Andrew felt a warm glow when he gave a large cheque to a deserving cause, but that alone was not enough to prise him away from the work he adored. He despised less sociable individuals, such as Jed Gardner. Every time they declined an invitation to meet potential customers, they were leaving money on the table.

Andrew and Lianne had been seated near a small chamber orchestra playing light classical tunes throughout the meal. When the speeches and presentation were over, Andrew turned to the musicians.

"A wonderful performance," he said, clapping his hands. He felt it was the least he could do. The minstrels had been hard at work while the charity's guests made merry with their fine food and wines.

The pretty blonde flute player blushed. "Not our best, I'm afraid," she said, "but we were only roped in this afternoon."

She looked familiar. "Haven't we met before?" he asked inquisitively.

"I don't think so," she said. "But I'm glad you liked us. Here's my card. We're available for corporate events and weddings, as well as classical music festivals." She dropped her voice. "Obviously, we played for free tonight, as it's a charity gig."

He was about to laugh, amused at her businesslike manner, when he glanced at her card. "Melissa Stevens," he read, recognising her at last. She was right; they had never met. He'd simply seen her picture in the papers. "You're Jed Gardner's girlfriend."

"Flatmate," she said promptly, correcting him, exactly as Lianne had been doing earlier with the other guests who had assumed she was his partner.

"I see," Andrew said, realising that he did not, at all. On the contrary, he was quite disconcerted by the news. His curiosity was rising. "Would you like to come to the opera with me next week?" he asked, on the spur of the moment. "La Bohème. We could meet for a drink in Covent Garden first."

"I'd love to," Melissa said. One of her friends was nudging her. She giggled. "I don't know your name, even."

"Do excuse my manners. Andrew Aycliffe. At your service." He bowed.

Melissa stopped smiling. "Andrew Aycliffe? I'm sorry; I don't think Jed would like that."

"He's not invited," Andrew said boldly, "and he doesn't need to know. Why should you tell him about it? You're not his girlfriend." He waited anxiously to see if she would have second thoughts.

"All right. We have a date, Andrew," Melissa said. "Let me know where you want to meet, but I think the Opera Tavern would suit me."

"Well, well," Lianne said, when they were both sharing the taxi he had booked to take him to his club and her on to Hampstead, "since when were you an opera buff?"

"Never," Andrew confessed. "A couple of Hundred Group CEOs asked me along."

"The Hundred Group? Is that another swanky gentlemen's club, or a secret society like the Freemasons?"

"Neither," Andrew said. "It's the largest companies in Britain: those listed on the FTSE100."

Lianne looked surprised. "Madrigal isn't in that league, is it?"

"No," Andrew admitted. "That's why, when I'm invited out with the big boys, I tend to accept. And I knew you were busy next week, so I couldn't ask you to be my plus one."

"You don't have to justify your date to me," Lianne retorted. "But she's surely not the little wifey you're looking for, is she?"

"She could be."

"No," Lianne said. "You're doing this to pay back Jed Gardner, aren't you?"

He shook his head, but he couldn't deny to himself that it was part of the attraction.

Chapter 30 Taylor's weekend without Boris

It was Spring Break, so Annie-Belle, a teacher, was free for lunch. "Thanks for fitting me into your busy schedule," she said.

"No problem." Taylor wasn't sure if Annie-Belle was being sarcastic or not. As it happened, her diary for the day was packed. She had taken an early train from Ambertown to New York's Penn Station, squeezing in two morning meetings with fashion magazines, and would be interviewed on radio that afternoon.

Annie-Belle twirled spaghetti around her fork with enthusiasm, but, Taylor noted, a total lack of competence. Strands escaped from Annie-Belle's fork and smeared sauce on her chin.

Annie-Belle realised too. "Pasta is a dish for girlfriends," she asserted, "and not one's fiancé."

Taylor understood that Annie-Belle's intention was to talk about her wedding. "Is your dress ready?" she asked.

"Yes, and it's awesome," Annie-Belle said proudly. "It's very simple and fitted, like, you know, Kate Middleton's style."

"Meringues are so last century," Taylor agreed.

Annie-Belle spent twenty minutes outlining her wedding plans in extreme detail, before finally asking Taylor if there was a man on the scene.

"One or two possibilities," Taylor said. Her mailbox had been glowing red-hot since her light-hearted article, 'My Weekend Without Boris Johnson', had been syndicated across the USA. Having discarded the weird, whacky and impoverished from the hundreds of men who had emailed her, she could take her pick from some very eligible bachelors.

"I loved your piece about those English losers," Annie-Belle said. "I guess you got something useful out of our trip to Europe, after all."

"Yes," Taylor said. "Especially as I never got paid by Airlite." Boris' bitcoins had been very useful to her, though, with airfares and other expenses to settle. She felt his dreadful behaviour justified a financial contribution.

"I'm not surprised," Annie-Belle said sympathetically. "I didn't suppose Martin Parsons would pay you, after you helped the US customs guys stake him out."

"Too right." Taylor shivered. "That was scary, hanging around for him with the suitcase in Times Square. I was surrounded by gunmen

118

waiting to ambush him. I was lucky the customs agent at JFK was so understanding. I could tell from the start that he believed me."

"He thought you were hot."

"He was cute," Taylor said. "Shame he couldn't give me his number. I can't even write about the case until it comes to trial, either. Did you know Martin Parsons was a fake? That wasn't his real name, and Airlite denied all knowledge of him."

"Those Brits were right; he was running a racket," Annie-Belle said.

"Not drugs, though but diamonds," Taylor said. "He set us up. I should have known the whole travel feature deal was too good to be true."

"Hey," Annie-Belle said, "talking of the British guys, did you hear about Boris Brooks and the GardNet Triangle?"

"Sure did," Taylor said cheerfully. That explained why Boris had stopped sending bitcoins, although, as a media celebrity, she scarcely needed them any longer. "Too bad for him. Those Europeans have a word to describe my feelings: Schadenfreude."

Chapter 31 Boris the traveller

"Are you sure you want more to drink?" the hostess asked.

"Absolutely," Boris replied. There was no point flying club class if he couldn't treat himself. "Another Glenfiddich, please." It was the only single malt stocked on the plane, and perfectly acceptable.

He sat back and relaxed as she served him without further comment. He was leaving behind the evils of the past, the furies unleashed when Melissa proposed and opened Pandora's Box: Lee's murder, the failed marriage, and his highly paid but hateful job. One day he would wave goodbye to whisky too; he was sure he could. For now, it was his constant companion.

He was flying to Zurich. There, a car would whisk him to Zug, twenty miles to the south. This especially low tax area of Switzerland, a tax haven within a tax haven, offered fiscal breaks to employees as well as foreign companies. Ironically, Boris didn't intend to stay there long.

Val had found him a modern flat, airy and glassy, a stone's throw from GardNet's new Swiss office. Boris had exchanged his Thames view for an Alpine vista. The office was located in a huge block of similar rooms. Boris could see from the brass plate by each door that they were rented to the Swiss branches of other large multinationals. The majority were devoid of life, their computers and telephones silent. Boris tutted as he walked past them, knowing most companies risked court action by HMRC for having so little substance in their Zug branches. By contrast, emails flowed like a river in and out of his workplace. Of course, GardNet was taking an even greater risk: Boris was the only signatory for the Swiss branch bank account.

He still found it hard to believe that Jed and Mark had agreed to it. Both appeared to want him in Switzerland for different reasons: Jed, because Boris' presence in London was a simple embarrassment, and Mark out of sympathy. It was true, too, that Mark's bonus would depend on the success of the tax planning; he wanted to do everything possible to make it work. That, Boris, supposed, was why Mark readily agreed when Boris asserted it was critical that only the local branch manager should have bank signature powers. Jed, who might be expected to jib at the arrangement, was in all likelihood unaware of it.

Mark obviously trusted Boris implicitly, and why should he not? Boris had never done anything underhand in the workplace, other than slip away early and inflate a few expense claims. Surely everyone did that? Mark was still a fool, nonetheless, a fool who deserved what was coming to him, Boris told himself. It was the CFO's actions in Amsterdam, his incitement to infidelity, that had caused the end of Boris' marriage.

A week into Boris' sojourn in Zug, Mark telephoned in evident panic. "Have you got all your companies yet, mate? Our shareholders want the cash tomorrow."

"We're good to go." Boris explained that the Swiss branch and Dutch company were already in place.

"We didn't need any Cayman entities then?"

"No," said Boris. He omitted to mention the five Caribbean companies registered at GardNet's expense. All were owned by him, as was another Swiss bank account. Probing his lawyers carefully for advice, he had confirmed that local secrecy laws precluded anyone from finding out.

"Great," Mark said, sounding relieved. "I'll tell the bank to move £80m tomorrow."

"OK," Boris said primly. "I'll do the paperwork at this end." Instead of using emails, he wrote and hand-delivered a letter to the bank, instructing them to transfer £80m from the Swiss branch to a trust in the Bahamas. There, as far as GardNet was concerned, the trail would go cold.

Several bank transfers later, £100,000 would emerge in Caz's bank account, another £100,000 in Diani's, and the balance in Boris' secret, numbered Swiss account. His conscience soothed by the thought of helping Kenyan orphans and Lee's family, Boris packed a suitcase and bought a rail ticket to Prague. He had heard it was the plastic surgery capital of Europe.

Chapter 32 Jed sees too much

Melissa was out with friends, having cocktails in Clapham. Jed missed her company. They usually either discussed, listened to or played music. He decided to turn to the television for his fix. Flicking the set on, he heard: "And now, live from the Royal Opera House, La Bohème."

While the orchestra tuned their instruments, the camera panned around the audience. Jed gasped. Melissa was sitting in one of the better seats, chatting animatedly to Andrew Aycliffe. He could not be mistaken. Aycliffe was stroking his beard, as he had done during their painful Project Shield negotiations. Melissa was wearing the pink dress in which she had left the flat earlier; the same pink dress, in fact, that she had worn to GardNet's Christmas party. They were both smiling.

Transfixed, he gawped at them. The camera could only have focused on them for seconds, but to Jed, it felt like hours. Eventually, the music began. He couldn't watch any longer. Switching off the TV, he concentrated on writing an algorithm to speed up GardNet's data transmission. Every ten minutes or so, he stopped and rang Jeannie, hoping for advice on what to say to Melissa when she came home. His calls went straight to voicemail.

Melissa did not return that night. He slept fitfully, half an ear open for the sound of her key in the lock, imagining too much and hating Aycliffe for it.

Chapter 33 Andrew's night at the opera

The lights dimmed and silence descended on the expectant audience. Music began. While Melissa watched the stage intently, Andrew found his mind wandering. Watching a Bond movie was more his style than La Bohème. He thought the opera's plot extremely flimsy, focused on a few fickle beauties and the sad men who danced attendance on them. He began to refine the sales pitch he had planned for the interval.

His companions were all older than him, large company CEOs in their forties and fifties with wives of a similar age. As champagne was served for the interval, the women enveloped Melissa in a cloud of conversation. By happy coincidence, they all seemed to have children who required music tuition. Andrew was free to concentrate on selling Madrigal's services.

The opera was significantly less frothy during its second half. The heroine was dying. To his alarm, Andrew noticed Melissa's eyes filling with tears. He had restricted his physical contact to a kiss on the cheek when they met for the evening, but of course he had hoped for more. Without a second thought, he reached out and squeezed her hand.

Melissa did not push him away, merely using her free hand to find a tissue and dab her tears. He gradually pulled her towards him. His arm was around her shoulders by the time the final act finished.

He had done enough networking, he decided. "You need to calm down," he whispered. "A drink will help, won't it? I'll take you to my club. It's quiet."

Melissa nodded.

Andrew said quick farewells to the group, and ushered Melissa through the surge of chattering punters leaving the Royal Opera House. Had he been alone he would have walked to his club, clearing his head in the night air, but he felt it would suit them both to be swiftly away from the crowds of Covent Garden. He hailed a taxi.

He was holding her hand again, lightly massaging it and enjoying the smooth feel of her skin. "Smile?" he suggested, as the cab whisked them away.

She managed a feeble, fleeting, grin. "I'm sorry," she said.

Andrew looked into her rich brown eyes, still beautiful despite their redness. "It's OK," he said. "It really is." He understood that women could be emotional, and just needed a sympathetic audience.

"Our time on this earth and our pleasures on it seem so short and fragile," Melissa said.

"We should enjoy it while we can," Andrew said. He hugged her. From the way she melted into his arms, he suspected Jed Gardner showed her little affection. After media reports of the GardNet Triangle, he was sure she must be in a relationship with Gardner, whatever she said. Evidently, the man was as glacial and unkind towards Melissa as he was in his business dealings. Why, after all, would she have agreed to a date if she were happy with Gardner? Andrew was even more determined to see the evening unfold as he had planned.

His club was no longer busy. It rarely was, once the post-work drinkers and diners had disappeared. Andrew found a shady corner in the bar and asked for a bottle of rosé champagne. While he preferred beer, he had discovered that, without exception, women adored pink fizz. It might bring Melissa's sparkle back too.

"I drank too much already," Melissa said, but she accepted a glass.

"Does that feel better?" he asked.

"Yes."

"Have some more and you'll feel even better."

Her eyes widened. "You know," she said, "this is the first time I've been out, just for fun, since..." Her voice tailed away.

"You need to unwind and have fun more often," Andrew said, putting his hand over hers and looking into her eyes. "Forget the past, forget your work. Live for the moment." As he said it, he realised it was very good advice, and perhaps he should even follow it himself. He poured more champagne.

The bottle was soon empty as they chatted about the opera and Melissa's life as a musician. Andrew was relieved she was beginning to relax again.

"Let's have some more," Andrew said. "I have a private room upstairs, by the way; would you like to see it? I can have drinks brought there."

"This would be a bedroom?" Melissa asked.

He couldn't divine her thoughts, but at least she didn't shrink back, and she was still holding his hand. "It's more than that," Andrew said. "Yes, there is a bed, but there's also a sitting area, and quite a pleasant view from the window."

"OK," Melissa said. "Why not? I'll check out that view."

The private room was the suite he usually booked: a bedroom with an antechamber containing a sofa, desk and chair. Andrew led Melissa to the sofa and sat next to her. He kissed her lightly on the lips.

He could tell from her response that she was attracted to him. He increased the pressure on her lips and gently caressed her hair and shoulders, moving his hands to her back and then her breasts.

Melissa reached up and stroked his hair, a tentative movement that nevertheless sent a shiver down his spine. Andrew desired her with a sudden intensity he had rarely experienced. All thoughts of Jed Gardner, and the hoped-for delight of spiting him, were banished. Urgently, he kissed Melissa with even more ardour, sweat beginning to prickle his brow. He unzipped her dress, unhooked her bra and slowly undressed her, his passion rising as he saw her creamy skin.

He pointed to the open bedroom door. "Shall we?" One hand leading her, the other unbuttoning his shirt and trousers with feverish haste, he took her to the huge white bed.

Andrew's figure was athletic, he knew, honed by regular swimming and gym workouts. He allowed himself a sense of pride as Melissa's eyes widened when his naked body was revealed.

Pulling her next to him, he sat on the bed. At first, he continued to kiss her mouth, but then turned his attention elsewhere. Sliding off the bed and kneeling before her, he kissed her inner thighs.

Melissa laughed, a merry sound. "I'm sorry," she gasped. "Your beard tickles. I'm not used to…"

"Hush," Andrew said. "I'll be more careful. Lie down." He didn't want her to say more, to compare him with Gardner or anyone else. He determined there and then to make it the best night of her life.

Melissa did as he asked, her blonde hair like a halo on the pillow. Andrew flicked his tongue across her inner thighs and the fair-haired mound above them, then over her belly to her torso, nipples and shoulders. He kissed her mouth again and lay on top of her, pushing her thighs apart and plunging inside.

He wasn't in a hurry. He moved rhythmically but slowly, stroking Melissa's hair and nipples and taking his pleasure from her reaction as passion spread within her. Only when he was sure she'd had her release did he allow himself to finish.

Melissa was happy, flushed and relaxed. Andrew smiled, gratified to have given her comfort. Tenderly, he kissed her lips once more. "Thank you," he said softly. "Will you stay?"

He expected her to agree, was in fact looking forward to a night simply cuddling her, so it was a rude shock when Melissa frowned and sat bolt upright.

"I should get back," she said. "It's late."

At those words and the apparent dissipation of her contentment, his thoughts returned to his cold rival and the opportunity to humiliate him. If only Melissa would stay. Although Gardner could not know she was with Andrew – that really would have twisted a knife into the man's guts – he would at least be unsettled by her absence.

He tried his most winning smile. "Please spend the night with me," he appealed.

"Yes, Andrew." She surrendered gracefully, with a kiss. When sleep claimed them, they were entwined in each other's arms.

Chapter 34 Jed's long day

Morning dawned grey, drizzly and far too early. Jed had overslept for the first time in well over a decade. It took a huge amount of willpower to rise from his bed. He made himself coffee and tried to work on his algorithm to distract himself. Music, which usually soothed his troubled soul, was out of the question. Every instrument, every note would bring his thoughts back to Melissa.

As the caffeine worked on him, his mind gained focus. He believed he had seen Melissa and Aycliffe on the TV screen, but what if he was wrong? Worse still, had Melissa travelled to Clapham and been the victim of a dreadful accident? Trembling, he dialled her number.

To her credit, she answered the phone. Much later, when he could bring himself to reflect, he realised it would have been easy for her simply to let it ring. She knew who was calling, for she said, "Hello, Jed."

"Where are you?" he asked, relieved at least that she was alive. He could hear muffled chatter in the background, and a male voice, surely Aycliffe's, asking her what was going on. Jed was certain he recognised the man's slightly nasal accent.

"I can't talk for long," she said. "I'm having breakfast."

"Who with?" He could not help it; his tone was reproachful. She would notice that.

"A friend." There was a long silence, then she said, "I think I should move out, Jed. You've been kind to let me have your spare room, but I can't take advantage of your hospitality forever."

Although she hadn't mentioned Aycliffe's name, Jed felt his worst fears were confirmed. "Where are you, Melissa?" he asked. "I'm getting a cab and coming over."

"It's a private club. They won't let you in." She sighed. "Are you at home? Stay there and I'll be right back."

It was again to her credit that she kept her word. Within thirty minutes, he heard the front door open. She was still wearing the pink dress, still heart-stoppingly beautiful.

"You spent the night with Aycliffe, didn't you?" he accused.

"How did you know?" She wouldn't meet his gaze, but even he, with his poor command of body language, could tell she was shocked.

"I saw you on TV," he snapped, unable to keep his rising anger in check.

Melissa gasped. "I'm sorry," she said. "I know you and he aren't exactly friends." At last, her brown eyes fixed on his, and he saw only turmoil within them.

"Melissa," his voice was tremulous. "If only it had been anyone but him. Anyone at all. And yet. I wish most of all it had been me."

She put a hand on his arm, and he was caught unawares by a rush of desire for her. He staggered backwards.

"You don't even want me to touch you," she said, completely misinterpreting his action. "You've never hugged me, even. You behave like a brother, and a distant one at that. Jed, it's a lover that I really need; someone who cares."

Jed's emotions were a maelstrom: dismay, anger and astonishment. He hardly knew what to say, but when words emerged from his lips, they sounded exactly right to him. "I care about you, Melissa, and that's why I've been patient," he said. "You told me you didn't want sex. I thought you just needed time. I wanted to be much more than a brother, or a friend." Her dalliance with Aycliffe was a bitter pill to swallow, but he knew he could find it within himself to forgive her. He took a deep breath. "That's still what I want, Melissa. Please stay."

She sat down, put her head in her hands. "I'm sorry, Jed," she said. "I don't know what I want, but I can't live here. I'm going to move back in with my parents."

He looked at her in bewilderment. "They're not in London are they, but your career is here – your concerts, your pupils, your music business contacts. How can you give all that up?"

"I won't," Melissa said. "My parents live in Brighton. I can commute." She shrugged. "I need space to decide what to do next."

"You don't have to go," he said, but he saw from her eyes that he had lost the battle. Shaken, and slightly unsteady on his feet, he packed his laptop and left for the taxi rank outside. He was already late for work, and was desperate for the comfort it offered. He would be consoled by the elegance of machine code, the boost to his confidence every time he cracked a supposedly insoluble problem. His profession would never abandon him, whereas he was certain that when he returned to St Pancras Chambers that evening, Melissa would no longer be there.

Raj and Mark were waiting in his office. "We have a ten o'clock meeting," Mark said, looking at his watch.

"Sorry."

"What is the world coming to?" Mark asked. "You not only arrive late at the office, but you apologise. Val tells me you've been leaving early too."

"It won't happen again," Jed said. "Shall we get down to business?"

"Sure," Raj said. "Let's start with some good news. Whitesmith are raving about the South Shields call centre. It's totally exceeded their expectations."

"Great," Mark said. "Will they reimburse us for the extra cost of running it?"

"They'll make a contribution towards it. However, I'm about to sign up two more big insurance clients," Raj said. "They want to use the South Shields call centre as well, and they'll pay handsomely for it."

"Do we have the capacity to service them?" Jed asked, concerned.

"We have the space, but not the people, so we'll have to recruit. That should attract good publicity; creating jobs in an unemployment blackspot."

Jed shuddered, remembering the last wave of publicity endured by GardNet. He was glad Eleanor was no longer capable of reading a newspaper; he could not hope to explain the GardNet Triangle to her.

"Best of all," Mark was saying, "our undertakings to Madrigal apply only to the current call centre staff. We can engage new call handlers on much lower pay."

"Well done, Raj," Jed said, and meant it. He began to feel more optimistic. His private life might be in pieces, but at least GardNet was growing its business.

"We need to talk about banking now, Jed," Mark said. "Our tax scheme goes live today. You'll recall that means a long chain of money transfers, starting with GardNet borrowing £80m from our bank and ending with our Swiss branch paying all of it to our shareholders."

"What is there to talk about?" Jed asked. "It's all in hand, isn't it?"

"Yes," Mark said. "I've personally approved instructions for all of the payments, except the last one. Boris is taking care of that."

"I hope he knows what he's doing," Jed muttered.

"He should do," Mark said cheerfully. "All he had to do was forward an email to the Swiss bank."

That set Jed's mind at rest. He gave the bank transfers no more thought until Mark called him just before four o'clock.

"£80m went into the Swiss branch at eleven o'clock," Mark explained, "but our shareholders claim they haven't received it."

"Tell their accountants to look harder," Jed said. "They're bound to have made a mistake."

"I'm not so sure," Mark mused. "Boris isn't answering phone calls and emails. I've tried to speak to our bank in Zug, but they won't tell me anything because only Boris has the authority to manage the account. I'm tempted to grab my passport and hop on a plane over there."

"Do just that," Jed said. "If you can't get a flight, ask Val to book a private jet. We have to know what's going on."

"Right."

As had been his habit until recently, Jed stayed behind at the office long after his colleagues had left for the evening. He was still there when Mark phoned at nine.

"It's not looking good," Mark admitted. "The office was deserted when I landed in Zug. Naturally, as it was so late. Then I tried Boris' flat."

"And?"

"He was out. I broke in, actually – picked the lock."

How, Jed wondered, had Mark learned to do that? He wasn't sure he respected his CFO's hidden talents.

Mark continued. "The place was in a state. Lots of empty whisky bottles, and I mean lots. At least half a dozen. He'd only been there a week."

"Are you convinced now that we should let him go?"

"Probably," Mark agreed. "There's worse, though, Jed. The cupboards were empty. He's left."

Jed's heart sank. "I bet ten to one, the money left with him."

"I can tell you're horrified, Jed. So am I," Mark said. "We can put pressure on the Swiss bank to tell us what's happened, but I'm inclined to think you're right. We'll find that the cash is gone, and I doubt it's simply hidden under Boris' mattress."

"That thieving little crook," Jed exploded. "I knew he'd be trouble. Why didn't you listen to me, Mark? We built this business from nothing, and now we've let Brooks bring it down." It was all too clear what this meant for GardNet's future, which that morning had looked so bright.

Mark's voice remained calm. "That leaves GardNet owing £80m to our shareholders still, and another £80m to our bank," he said, as if reading Jed's mind. "It's a very high level of debt - almost unsustainable. I'm sorry, Jed, it's touch and go whether the company will go under." He paused. "Our shareholders may save the day, though at a price. The business is motoring ahead, so I think they'll support it."

Jed knew Mark well enough to understand the nuances in that statement.

"And what about you and me, Mark?" In his heart, he already knew the answer.

Mark sighed. "They're hard-nosed private equity entrepreneurs. Why should they be kind to us? When I say there's a price to be paid, I'm telling you who'll pay it. It's the two of us, mate. We'd better polish our CVs."

Chapter 35 Andrew plays his cards right

Having treated Melissa to breakfast at his club, Andrew extracted from her a promise to meet him for dinner the following week, then left for Shoreditch and a long day at the office. He drove back to Birmingham late that evening, and was ensconced in his office there when Scott Georgeson phoned the next day.

"It's been a long time since we spoke," the headhunter said.

"Indeed. What have you been doing in the last seven years?" Andrew had little to thank the man for, but he saw no harm in being polite.

"More of the same," Scott said. "I'm doing some fascinating work for private equity houses now."

"Aren't they notoriously tight-fisted? How do you make it pay?"

Scott chuckled. "I achieve excellent results. My clients pay for quality. In that context, I've been asked to sound you out about an exciting opportunity that might arise soon. You're based in Birmingham now, aren't you? How do you feel about going back to London?"

"Out of the question," Andrew said. "I work in London one or two days a week at the moment, and that's quite enough." Impulsively, he added, "Why doesn't your client relocate to Birmingham? We've saved a fortune at Madrigal by having our HQ here rather than paying for overpriced premises in Mayfair. It's crazy how some companies throw cash away. I mean, your old friend Jed Gardner uses helicopters like taxis. GardNet must be paying a pretty penny for that."

Scott was silent.

"Hello? Are you still there?" Andrew asked.

"You raised an interesting point," Scott said. "I'll put it to my client."

"I'd like to catch up," Andrew said, "but my London diary's booked solid for weeks. Why don't you visit Brum? It's only an hour from Euston and you'll be pleasantly surprised. It's not all slagheaps north of Watford, you know."

He looked out of the window at St Paul's Church, glowing blinding white in the spring sunshine, surrounded by candyfloss puffs of cherry blossom. Madrigal's offices were in the old Jewellery Quarter of the city, which had incredibly survived Hitler's bombs and the Sixties planners unscathed. Andrew had bought a flat nearby when he first started work at Madrigal. Although he now lived in considerable style a couple of miles away, he still retained his affection for the area. He saw no point in leaving it, or the job he loved.

"How about lunch tomorrow?" Scott asked.

"I have an existing commitment."

"The day after, then."

He must be serious. Andrew immediately agreed. The best restaurant nearby served delicious curries. Andrew, regretfully, decided that a curry in Birmingham was too clichéd, serving only to confirm a Londoner's prejudices about the city. Instead, he booked a table at Purnell's, a Michelin starred establishment halfway between his office and the railway station where Scott would be arriving from London.

At the appointed hour, Andrew was late: deliberately. He found Scott already seated and looking with approval around the room, modern and sleek in grey and black. "This will be on me," he offered.

"I won't argue," Andrew said.

"I've followed your career with interest," the headhunter said, as they ordered sparkling mineral water before studying the menu. "Could you tell me, in your own words, what you think you've achieved at Madrigal, and why you want to stay there?"

Andrew outlined his junior role when he first joined the family-owned business, his rapid promotion and the company's growth since it was floated on the London Stock Exchange. Madrigal was known within the industry for offering a great quality of life to its staff. One of the reasons, Andrew explained, was that both he and the Armstrongs believed in sharing the benefits of the company's success with the people that made it possible. Andrew had bought a huge house in one of Birmingham's premier suburbs; twice a year, marquees were erected in the garden and all of Madrigal's employees bussed in for a Christmas party and a summer bash.

"You could do that in London," Scott pointed out.

"I choose not to," Andrew said patiently. "Quite apart from the cost, I like it here. Our customers don't care where our offices are, as long as we send engineers to them swiftly when they've got a problem."

"Is it just the location that keeps you at Madrigal?"

"No, it is working with great people and also being there to support them. That's why I'm unlikely to accept your client's offer."

"That's a pity," Scott said. "Frankly, I think my client would be receptive to moving their HQ here. They're a very dynamic company, but they're in a spot of bother with their finances. It means they have to cut costs, and one possibility is leaving London. Not that financial constraints override their recruitment needs. The shareholders want to replace their entire management team, and they'll make it worthwhile for the right candidate. They've already identified you as the frontrunner."

"Can I ask who they are?" Andrew asked cautiously.

"If you keep it strictly confidential." Scott looked around the room, anxiously ruffling his waxed hair. He lowered his voice to a whisper. "The company is GardNet. My client, technically, is not GardNet itself, but their private equity shareholders. They have had to make some tough decisions. The result is that Jed and Mark will be resigning, but they don't know yet."

Andrew was puzzled. "How come? I hear on the grapevine that GardNet is doing really well. I'm beginning to regret selling that call centre to them."

"As I said," Scott kept his voice low, "their financial situation is poor. The company is about to be reconstructed by the shareholders and their banks. Reading between the lines, there's been a fraud, and the feeling is that Jed Gardner and Mark Trelawney are to blame. They'll be asked to resign and give up their minority shares as well. You hit the nail on the head when you said GardNet splashes cash around. There will be some big spending cuts, starting with Jed Gardner's company flat. New management will be imposed as soon as we can recruit them."

"I'm on a year's notice," Andrew pointed out, "and I would intend to honour it."

"I can help Madrigal recruit a successor," Scott smirked.

"I bet you could." Andrew laughed. "All right. I'll talk to your client, and if we can agree terms, I will do my best to negotiate an early release from Madrigal's board."

Andrew couldn't believe the irony. Having almost destroyed GardNet, he was now being asked to run it. He suspected Jed Gardner would be devastated. He was not sorry. Although he would never admit it to Scott, it was a factor in his decision to talk to the headhunter's client.

Within a week, Andrew was seeing the shareholders of GardNet. They were genuinely considering moving its head office, currently a stone's throw from the Bank of England, to Birmingham. He made sure of that by insisting on meeting them in the second city. Their discussion was a sombre one, held in a room at one of the anonymous hotels that ringed the International Convention Centre. There, Andrew learned there had indeed been a fraud.

"GardNet has a tax manager called Boris Brooks." The speaker was Darryl Danville, younger even than Andrew and introduced to him as chief operating officer of Stargate, the private equity house.

"I've heard," Andrew observed.

Danville's mouth crinkled at the corners. "Those GardNet Triangle stories, no doubt? We may suppose that Mr Brooks did not like Mr Gardner much. It's unfortunate, then, that Gardner allowed Brooks to set up a tax structure that involved channelling £80m in cash through a bank account to which Brooks was the sole signatory."

"That's exactly what GardNet paid for Madrigal's call centre," Andrew said.

Danville's finance colleague, a Canadian woman called Angie Ross, chipped in. "We thought GardNet had overpaid, to be frank, but we decided to let it go. Their tax structure made the economics much more attractive."

She was older than Danville, in her forties, with features that had settled into a determined expression. Despite her artfully styled dark hair and smart red suit, Andrew surmised she could be quite scary.

"I feel I negotiated a good price for Madrigal," he said carefully. "Let me guess what happened to the money once it went into the account controlled by Brooks."

"Your guess is as good as ours," Danville said. "We know the money went into the account, and after a degree of arm twisting, we finally had the bank's confirmation that it came out. We don't know where it went. Nor, in fact, do we know the whereabouts of the elusive Mr Brooks. It's safe to say there have been major control failures at GardNet, and we believe their executive board should be replaced. That, incidentally, means Jed Gardner and Mark Trelawney must leave. As well as being directors, they are minority shareholders. They own part of the business. But that stake is worthless, as GardNet is technically insolvent thanks to the actions of Mr Brooks."

"We will require them to sell their shares to us for one pound, as well as resign," Angie Ross said. "Stargate has lent GardNet £80m, and we will convert that loan into shares. We're being required to do so by the company's bankers."

Andrew was happy to agree that Jed Gardner should leave. Mark Trelawney was a different matter. He bore no ill will towards the GardNet CFO. "I think we should give Mark Trelawney a chance to explain himself, and to stay with GardNet," he said.

"Impossible," Angie Ross said. "The fraud happened because he allowed it. He made an error of judgement in recruiting Boris Brooks, and compounded it with control weaknesses."

"I believe everyone learns from their mistakes," Andrew said, "apart from a few exceptions, like Jed Gardner." Gardner, it appeared, had never gathered that it was stupid to antagonise people. While he couldn't condone the fraud, Andrew felt on balance that his sympathies lay with Boris Brooks.

Angie Ross laughed lightly. "Yes, Jed is rather an abrasive character, isn't he? An IT genius, but I'm afraid we can't keep either him or Trelawney. They've lost the confidence of our bankers."

"Let me talk to the bankers, and Mark Trelawney," Andrew offered. "Perhaps I can change their minds."

"I think Angie needs to be with you when that happens," Danville said. "And I want to see Messrs Gardner and Trelawney first. Stargate hasn't communicated its plans to them yet, and nor will we do so until they are firm. For instance, we must know if you're coming on board. So tell us what you'd do for us to cut costs at GardNet and prepare the business for a stock market flotation."

"I'd sell the lease on their pricy offices, and Gardner's flat," Andrew said, "and move from London. Nothing in that to scare the horses – am I right?" He looked at their faces and saw confirmation, before continuing. "More controversially, I'd increase headcount in the UK. Why? Because customer satisfaction surveys reveal that people want local IT support. I see from the industry press that GardNet is signing more clients because it has a UK call centre. I'll grow that top line by making it a virtue among their clients to buy British."

"What about salary costs?" Angie Ross asked sharply. "Is it true that Madrigal pays 10% above the industry average?"

"We pay to recruit and retain the best people," Andrew said, "and it works. Look at Madrigal's growth."

"I think you already know we'd like some of that," Danville said. "So what will it take to tempt you to GardNet?"

Andrew named a figure, and repeated that he would have to negotiate an exit date with his board colleagues at Madrigal. They would need time to recruit a successor. In fact, he was confident this would be straightforward. There were at least two internal candidates who, with a bit of coaching, would be ready to run the company. He resolved to ask Lianne if she could help them.

Andrew had postponed his London office day to the end of the week. He rang Melissa and asked whether, instead of dinner, she would like to stay with him in Birmingham for the weekend. She readily agreed, saying she had studied at the Conservatoire, and she would love to revisit old haunts. That was how he came to be driving her up the M1 on Friday night in his red rocket.

"Do you like the car?" he asked, pressing hard on the gas pedal and enjoying the engine's agreeably throaty roar as it pulled forward.

Melissa nodded. "It's fun," she said. "I never learned to drive, and nor did Boris. There was no need in London."

"Boris?"

"My ex. Boris Brooks."

He seized his chance. "What's Boris doing now?" he asked, careful to make the enquiry sound nonchalant.

She shivered. "I don't know. He's signed the divorce papers, and that's all I care about. I want a clean break. He can keep his flat, his bank account and his blue movie collection. I never want to see him again."

He would learn nothing of value from her. Stargate would just have to hope their private investigators found Brooks before he spent all his ill-gotten gains.

He concentrated on charming her. Initially attracted to Melissa by her looks, and then the sweet delight of stealing her from Gardner, he was starting to like her a great deal and wished to know her better. The quicker he drove, the sooner he would lead her into his bedroom and onto his wide four poster bed. They could continue what they had started on the soft linen sheets of the room at his club.

"What were your student days like?" he asked.

"I shared a flat in Edgbaston with Alexa. You met her at the Orangery. She was playing first violin."

Andrew's recollection of the other musicians was blurred. "I live in Edgbaston too. Farquhar Road."

137

"I know it." Melissa's eyes sparkled. "It's the best address in Birmingham. Well, the Edgbaston where I lived was very different from Farquhar Road. I could have cycled between them in ten minutes, but they were light years apart. I lived in a leaky concrete block near the Edgbaston Reservoir. It was amazingly cheap, but with good reason. There were rodents. We couldn't afford heating, so we stayed at the Conservatoire as long as possible, or went to pubs to keep warm."

Andrew sympathised. "It sounds like my early life. Apart from the pubs."

He had lived in a tall sixties tower at the very edge of the city, draughts whistling through it whenever the wind blew, until his father's job prospects improved enough for the family to buy a rundown house in a poor area. His university years, by contrast, had been spent in halls of residence that appeared to be a byword for luxury. Although cramped, his room had been heated to a subtropical degree.

"Surely it would cost less to heat your flat than buy drinks?" he suggested.

"Not if you make half a pint last all night. Or someone else is buying the drinks. I met Boris then. He was very generous and his flat was toasty."

That was the basis on which she had chosen a life partner. Andrew was relieved that his property would be comfortably warm when they arrived. Using his smartphone, he could control the temperature, lights, curtains and music, even from the other side of the world. He had taken the precaution of adding a few classics to his usual playlist of Britpop.

Melissa admired the house and insisted on a tour. Finally, Andrew took a bottle of chilled champagne and two glasses to his bedroom. Melissa followed, kissing him on the lips and willingly complying with his plans for the evening.

His dreams were sweet that night. He was up early as usual, leaving her to sleep while he plunged into the clear blueness of his pool. He mused idly about Melissa's suitability as a wife. She would be an asset if he needed to take a partner to a business function. He knew too, through gentle questioning, that she liked children. He should start a family sooner rather than later, if he wanted to be sure he would see his children grow up.

His father's early death had been a grim reminder of Andrew's own mortality. Impelled to keep fit, he swam twenty lengths, refreshing himself for a long day ahead. The interviews of the past week had robbed him of time he could scarcely spare, and he ought to do some work before Melissa awoke.

He did not finish his tasks, and suggested he stayed at home while Melissa went sightseeing. The city had changed a great deal since she was a student, he told her. They could meet later near Symphony Hall. Andrew had been obliged to call in favours to secure a pair of tickets for a performance there. Having never been to one of their concerts before, he had been surprised to find the City of Birmingham Symphony Orchestra always sold out months ahead.

"Why didn't you stay here and join the CBSO?" he asked, as they ate their supper in a French restaurant overlooking a canal. The evening sunshine had turned the water to liquid gold. Upon it, ducks bobbed and brightly coloured barges glided past.

"I applied, but without success," Melissa said, with commendable frankness. "They don't need many flautists." She shrugged. "It was the same story with the Manchester Hallé and the big London orchestras. I may have been unlucky. Who knows? Alexa was in a similar position, so we set up our own chamber orchestra."

"And the rest is history," Andrew said. Hardly a classical buff, he couldn't really judge whether they were of a sufficiently high standard for the CBSO or not. They had certainly sounded pleasant enough at the Orangery.

"It's not an easy vocation, though," Melissa said. "Alexa and I both give lessons to make ends meet. And if it wasn't for Boris, Jed, and now my parents, I'd be living in a rat-infested garret again."

"You like this city, don't you?" Andrew said impetuously. "If you lived here, we could see more of each other. I still own a loft apartment, actually, near my office. You could live there. It's hardly a freezing attic." In his mind's eye, he pictured a love nest: champagne in the fridge, mirrors in the bedroom, and a warm greeting from Melissa when he crossed the threshold.

"A rich man's mistress in a little flat?" Melissa said, amused. "That isn't me. Anyway, my work is in London."

He forbore from asking her what she thought she'd been to Gardner and Brooks. Brooks at least had cared enough to marry her. Who knew what Gardner's motives were? While Andrew admired Gardner's good taste, his hatred of the man was undiminished. He allowed himself to gloat at the arrogant CEO's impending downfall.

The weekend passed all too quickly, especially as Andrew had arranged a board meeting on Monday to tell his fellow directors that he intended to leave Madrigal. He was not looking forward to the conversation, but in any event, the meeting went well. His colleagues agreed with plans for his succession, and he was able to tell Darryl Danville that he would be joining GardNet in three months' time.

The news was followed by a telephone call from Angie Ross. "I've arranged to see Mark Trelawney tomorrow," she told him.

"Too bad," Andrew said. "I won't be in London until Thursday." He intended to make a point, and make it early. Stargate needed to understand that he was doing business with them on his own terms.

"We can't approach Gardner until Trelawney's future is resolved," the Canadian said. "Nor can we make your involvement public."

"A few days makes no difference to you," Andrew said. "GardNet is hardly likely to fall victim to another fraud in that time, so you may as well let Gardner and Trelawney run it. I, on the other hand, have plenty to do at Madrigal before Thursday."

She agreed; reluctantly, Andrew thought. She had little choice, though, and they both knew it. He held all the cards. Stargate not only wanted GardNet rescued from insolvency, they wanted it to grow and become a public company. He was one of a handful of individuals who could deliver that.

The meeting with Mark Trelawney was held on neutral ground, at Andrew's instigation. Angie Ross invited GardNet's CFO to have breakfast with her at Andrew's club. Once pleasantries were over, and Mark had been plied with coffee and allowed to recover from his surprise at Andrew's presence, Angie cut to the chase.

"You may be aware that Stargate has done its own investigations into GardNet's failure to repay our loan," she informed Mark in her clipped Canadian accent. "We have confirmed that Boris Brooks has absconded with £80m. GardNet is technically insolvent as a result."

Mark rose to his feet. "I don't think it's appropriate to discuss GardNet's financial position in front of him," he said, pointing at Andrew.

"Sit down, Mark," Angie said. She smiled. "Andrew is GardNet's new CEO. It's not official yet, so keep it confidential, huh?"

Andrew's respect for her grew. Her friendly expression had not quite reached her eyes, he noticed. She was a smart cookie.

Mark gawped at Andrew, curtly said, "Congratulations," and sat down again.

"So, GardNet's finances are in the red," Angie recapped. "Stargate's proposals for curing this are, firstly, that we convert our loan to equity. As a precondition, we ask that you and Jed Gardner sell your shares to us for £1. The company will then be 100% owned by us."

"I won't agree to that, and I doubt Jed will either," Mark said. "Why should we?"

Angie repeated her half-smile. "I think you should both agree, because we'll call in the liquidators if you don't. You should also be aware that, for at least two weeks, GardNet has been trading while insolvent. Stargate will press the liquidator to make a claim against you for wrongful trading. All your personal assets could be seized and you could be disqualified as a director."

For a fleeting moment, Andrew thought she was bluffing. Mark, however, must have been convinced otherwise. His shoulders slumped.

"Very well," he said. "I'm sure I can persuade Jed."

Angie nodded. "Secondly," she said, "we will be requiring Jed to resign. There has been some debate, too, over your position at the company, Mark."

"You mean I should be treating this as a job interview?" Mark asked. He turned to Andrew. "What would you like to know?"

"Only one thing," Andrew said, relieved that Mark was so astute. He was confident they could work well together. "I don't care why you recruited Brooks, or why you allowed him to help himself to £80m. That's water under the bridge. You know what went wrong, and you can fix it. What I really need is your confirmation that you'll move back to the Midlands, because that's where GardNet's offices are going to be."

Mark gasped. "My wife's job is in London," he said. "I can't possibly expect her to give it up."

"You've got 24 hours to decide," Andrew said. Mark was no idiot. Once he had considered his options, he would realise how limited they were.

Stargate swiftly arranged for Andrew to meet GardNet's bankers. They, too, agreed that Mark would remain in post and Andrew would supplant Jed. Within days, the news was all over the financial press.

Without a pang of pity, Andrew gazed at pictures of Jed leaving GardNet's offices, a bin liner in his hand and a forlorn expression on his face.

Chapter 36 Boris returns

Boris left Prague with a cleft chin, killer cheekbones and a German ID card announcing his identity as Herr Florian Berg. Whether it was lost or stolen, he did not know, but he had no difficulty gaining entry to Britain at Heathrow.

"Your English is very good," commented the immigration clerk to whom Boris had wished a cheery 'Good afternoon'.

"I went to boarding school here," Boris said, his story ready.

He caught a glimpse of his reflection in a large window, and barely recognised himself. His blond hair was close cropped to his skull, almost shaved. He sported a moustache and dark glasses. After liposuction, his figure was considerably more athletic and flattered further still by Armani.

He dosed himself with whisky to quell the regret he felt at the knowledge that he would never see his sister or friends again, or even Melissa. Especially Melissa. Still, he had already found it easy to attract women. His stag weekend had been but the nursery slopes. Smirking, he recalled a recent night in Prague, when he had celebrated the removal of bandages from his face. Throwing an outrageous sum of money around in a nightclub, he had attracted not just one gorgeous woman to accompany him to his hotel, but three. It seemed that size really did not matter.

Initially, he had planned to retire to the Caribbean, but he'd been away from London for so long, he found himself hankering for it. Surely with his new look and identity, he could afford to return just one more time? Booking a room at the Hilton on Park Lane, he soon found agreeable female company in the rooftop bar. Kristina was blonde, stunning, and delighted to meet him. Boris decided he would spend a few days of unbridled hedonism with her.

Chapter 37 Szymon's luck

"Another drink?" Szymon was in a generous mood.

Ravi waved him away. "Not for me. I must go home; I've got an essay to write."

"Go on," Szymon urged. "I owe you one."

Ravi laughed. "I've had my 10%, and I'm happy with that. I told you they'd settle quickly, didn't I?"

"Four months? Is that quick?"

"Yes, for the UK. Some legal cases take nearly a decade to resolve. We did well. I think you're pleased with the size of your payout, too."

Szymon nodded. Ravi had secured twice as much compensation as he initially estimated. There was every reason to celebrate.

"Well," Ravi said, placing a slim hand on Szymon's stocky shoulder, "I'll see you later. Look after him." The last remark was directed to Szymon's friends, Piotr and Lech.

They waved goodbye.

"I'll get some more beers in," Szymon said jovially. "Better than homebrew, eh?"

"My homebrew's not bad," Piotr retorted. "It does the job of getting me drunk, anyway."

"His is too fizzy and sweet," Lech said, pointing to Szymon.

"Piotr's recipe," Szymon grumbled in protest. He caught a waiter's eye and ordered six bottles of Tyskie. "Two each."

"That's definitely to my liking," Lech said. "A long day on that building site works up a thirst." He took a swig and lit a roll-up.

They were sitting outside the bar, in a cobbled alleyway just off Oxford Street. The party mood continued as they enjoyed the last rays of the day's sunshine. Although dusk was falling, the air was balmy.

"Hey," Szymon nudged Piotr, "Look at the size of those."

All three men stared at the couple drinking cocktails at the next table, surrounded by shopping bags from exclusive boutiques. "Do you mean the size of these," Piotr asked, cupping his hands and holding them in front of his chest, "or the size of those?" He gestured to the ground with one hand and the sky with the other.

"Both," Szymon said. The beautiful blonde girl was not only well-endowed, but much taller than her companion. For some reason he couldn't fathom, a picture of Melissa and Boris swam into his mind. He

144

shook his head, hoping to dislodge the thought. This was a time for fun, not angry memories of that lying asshole.

The woman noticed their collective gaze. She whispered to the man. It was not possible altogether to discern his thoughts, as he wore wraparound sunglasses, but the set of his mouth looked distinctly unfriendly.

Szymon shivered. There was a hint of menace about the short man. Perhaps he was a gangster. Szymon began to prepare a grovelling apology to use if the atmosphere took a turn for the worse.

It was when the man opened his mouth that Szymon nearly fell off his chair.

"Who are you looking at?" the man growled.

Szymon recognised the timbre. It was unquestionably that asshole's voice. How could this be? The man looked completely different. Gradually, Szymon spotted similarities in height, hair colour and posture. Boris Brooks must have simply lost a lot of weight.

Momentarily forgetting his compensation, and the fact that working as a concierge had bored him to distraction, Szymon allowed himself to feel righteous indignation. That spiteful little liar had caused him to lose a job that he loved. Worse, now he was encroaching on Szymon's right to have a peaceful beer with his friends. Mr Brooks had undoubtedly arrived here with the express intention of causing trouble for Szymon once again.

He would not stand for it. All fear left him as he rose unsteadily to his feet, and, towering over Brooks, said, "What's your problem?"

Brooks recoiled in shock, and Szymon was certain that the short man had identified him and realised a fight was brewing. He wasn't the only one, for the waiter sprang between them and told them that, if they wished to argue, they must leave the premises.

"I don't wish to argue with anyone," Brooks said, brandishing a twenty pound note.

Szymon could tell from the young waiter's expression that he would dearly love to accept it, but the fear of violence outweighed his avarice. "No, no, you must both leave," the young man said once more.

Szymon shrugged. "I'm going. Come on, guys."

"Why should we?" Piotr complained. "What's wrong with appreciating beauty, anyway?"

"Come on," Lech hissed. "Or he'll call the police."

At the mention of police, Brooks began to fidget. "All right, I'll drink elsewhere," he said hastily, replacing the note in his wallet. "Come on, Kristina. Hurry up." He picked up her shopping bags and ushered her away.

"What was that about?" Piotr asked.

"That's the asshole who got me fired," Szymon said bitterly.

"No way," Piotr exclaimed. "Then we should teach him a lesson."

They followed Brooks and his paramour to a side street, this one deserted and lined with shuttered shops and offices.

"Go on," Piotr said, digging an elbow in Szymon's ribs, "you'll take him out easily."

Szymon took a run at Brooks, headbutting him. Brooks fell back onto the pavement, bloody-nosed and winded. His broken sunglasses lay beside him, his companion's shopping bags scattered on the ground.

The girl screamed harsh words in a language they didn't understand, then swung her handbag at Szymon's head. At the same time, Brooks gingerly lifted himself from the pavement and punched Szymon's stomach.

Buoyed by adrenaline, Szymon hardly noticed the pain. His friends, however, were not idle. They rushed to his aid. Lech grappled with the blonde for her handbag. Piotr, still holding a beer bottle, brought it down on Brooks' crown. There was a cracking sound. Brooks keeled over, blood pouring from his head as well as his face.

At the sight of the bottle and blood, the blonde yelped in panic, grabbing her bag from Lech's now unprotesting hands. Stopping briefly to pick up her shopping, she fled, high heels clattering.

The adrenaline rush subsided. "What now?" Szymon asked. "She may be calling the cops."

Piotr laughed dirtily. "Not her type. We've no worries there. On the other hand, if we leave this piece of shit lying in the street, he'll attract attention. Look," he pointed to an alleyway, almost blocked with huge trade waste bins, "let's take him there, so nobody will trip over this mess."

They dragged the bloodied, unconscious man to the alley, obviously a waste area for the commercial premises in the street.

"Pah," Piotr said. "He doesn't weigh much. You know, he appeared to have plenty of cash. Let's take a look." He felt around Brooks' jacket.

"Here we are, a lovely fat wallet. He doesn't need this for his night out any more." He began to remove the contents.

"He's a German," Lech observed, as Piotr brandished an ID card.

"That man is as German as..as..as the Pope," Szymon said drunkenly. "What does that credit card say? Florian Berg? No way is it his real name." He waved magnanimously at the wallet. "You split the cash between you, guys. I'll take the cards."

"Are you sure?" Piotr asked. "There's a thousand pounds here."

"Quite sure," Szymon said, brushing away any thoughts of remorse as he planned the shopping spree he would enjoy with Brooks' credit card.

"You know," Piotr said thoughtfully, "this asshole is still too obtrusive. Let's just stick him out of the way in one of those bins."

Brooks moaned, clearly not as lifeless as they had thought.

"Quick, he's about to wake up and make trouble for us. Throw him into that one," Szymon said, pointing at the nearest bin. "I'll help you." He gave Brooks a gratuitous cuff across his head before they slammed the lid shut.

"Time for another drink," Piotr said. "A big one."

"Good idea," Szymon said. "Why don't we go back to mine for some homebrew?" He decided he had seen enough of the West End.

Lech chuckled. "You know what we think of your brewing skills."

"We can go to my flat," Piotr said. "My girlfriend's away for a couple of days."

Piotr had moved away from Beckton to Walthamstow. The three men strolled to Oxford Circus to take the Victoria Line.

"What time is it?" Szymon moaned groggily, as Piotr's alarm clock cut through his sleep the next morning. It couldn't be that early, as bright sunshine streamed through the flimsy curtains. Stretching his limbs, he immediately regretted it. He was lying on a sofa, head throbbing and joints stiff. Beside him in the cramped studio, Piotr and Lech lay at opposite ends of a double bed.

"6 am, the same time I always get up, and you too, I'm sure," Piotr said, sitting bolt upright without an apparent trace of hangover. "Come on, Lech." He shook his friend awake.

"Tell the boss I'm sick," Szymon begged. Even with painkillers, he couldn't begin to handle heavy loads at the site.

Piotr shrugged. "It's up to you, friend. No work, no pay."

Szymon envied Piotr's strong constitution. The electrician was younger than Szymon, of course, but he also habitually drank more and perhaps that was why so much beer had no effect on him. Abandoning his friends to their Tube journey, Szymon found a cafe on Hoe Street prepared to serve him coffee and a greasy bacon sandwich. The local news was on the radio, and he was relieved to hear no mention of Florian Berg, Boris Brooks or a man left in a waste skip. Such events were, of course, commonplace in London, so it didn't mean Brooks hadn't been discovered. Desperately drinking more coffee to sober up, he fumbled in his pocket for Brooks' dubious ID and credit card.

How long would it be before Brooks recovered and put a stop on the credit card? Szymon decided he should use it quickly, preferably just for that morning. On impulse, he tried one of the bank ATMs on Hoe Street. Of course, he would need to deduce Brooks' PIN number. Aware the card could be retained by the cash machine if he made too many bad guesses, Szymon resolved to have two goes only. Luck was with him. Brooks had used one of the most common combinations: 1234. Having first tried 1111, Szymon was successful on the second attempt.

The ATM would only disgorge £500. Disgruntled, Szymon wandered around the nearby shopping streets. It was too early for most establishments to be open, and anyway, they didn't stock the high value, portable items he was hoping to buy and sell on to his acquaintances. He was on the point of heading for the Tube when he noticed the betting shop. A young man, trim in a dark suit, was just unlocking the door.

"You're too early," he said, detecting Szymon's interest. "Ten minutes."

"Just one question," Szymon said. "Can you make me rich?"

"It's possible. Depends what you're prepared to stake."

"£500," Szymon said boldly.

The man whistled. "You could win a hundred grand with an accumulator on the horses. Up for it?"

"Yes." Why not? He had hoped to obtain serious money from Brooks' card, enough to persuade Marta to take him back. £500 was clearly insufficient. £100,000, on the other hand, was a fortune, the sort of money he'd hoped to earn when he took a bus to London with his pretty young wife several years before.

"All right." The man grinned. "Come inside, and you can place the bet at opening time. What would you like – a straight accumulator, a Yankee, a Canadian or what?"

Szymon gawped at him.

"I know," the young man said kindly, "I'll do you an accumulator and we'll stick to the favourite in each race, OK?"

Szymon handed over the cash, the notes crisp and clean. "My name is Berg," he said. "Florian Berg." He flashed the ID card in case it was required. The photograph on it was of poor quality and could be almost anybody. Doubtless, that was why Brooks had been using it.

Taking his betting slip, Szymon took the Tube to central London and walked along Tottenham Court Road. While he had never been in the market for high end gadgets, he had heard this was the place to buy them. He had spent nearly £20,000 on premium branded products from Apple, Sony and Samsung before the card was declined.

He could sell some of the items casually, to other site workers and a few of his friends. The best prices, though, would be realised online. Szymon recalled that, as well as her cleaning job, Anna ran a sideline selling goods on eBay. She sometimes sat at the kitchen table packaging them: books, items of clothing and small trinkets. Szymon didn't know how she obtained them. Some were undoubtedly given to her by domestic clients. The new garments, still with tags attached, might have been shoplifted. He wasn't sure how she'd react if he approached her with the goods he had just bought. Surely he'd be doing them both a favour if he asked her to sell them for a small commission? He resolved to canvass Andrzej's views that evening. Meanwhile, he threw the now useless card down a storm drain.

Although it was the middle of the day, he was still aching and fatigued. He returned to Beckton, lay on his narrow bed, and immediately fell asleep.

His room was in darkness when he awoke. At first, Szymon blinked, disorientated. There was no window to hint at the time of day; indeed, he had no idea whether it was day or night. Eventually, he noticed the thin line of sunlight under the shabby plywood door. He looked at his watch as his eyes adjusted to the dim light. It was already seven o'clock.

Szymon stumbled downstairs to the kitchen. Anna and Andrzej were eating supper, a fragrant stew red with tomatoes and peppers. The savoury smell set Szymon's mouth watering. He remembered his last meal had been a bacon sandwich in Walthamstow. Nevertheless, his hunger was outweighed by curiosity about the racing results.

"Have you seen Ravi?" he asked.

"Should I have?" Anna looked at him coldly. "Did you leave the bathroom tap running this morning?"

"No." Szymon's expression was one of injured innocence. "I wasn't here this morning."

She rolled her eyes, then returned to stabbing a lump of meat with her fork. Szymon walked upstairs again and knocked on Ravi's door.

"Who is it?"

"Szymon. Can I check something on your computer?"

"Go ahead." Ravi opened the door to him. Szymon looked around. The room was spacious and neat, smelling of sandalwood. Ravi had the luxury of a double bed to himself, a wardrobe and a well-filled bookcase as well as the inevitable shoddy computer desk and chair. On the desk sat a Sony laptop and a fan, clicking and whirring. The window, which would have permitted entry to Beckton's overripe summer air, was firmly shut.

"Please. Sit down and take your time," Ravi said, gesturing at the desk. "I'm already online."

Laboriously, Szymon compared his runners with the results on the Racing Post website, his excitement mounting at every reported win.

"Well, that looks like good news for you," Ravi said, obviously clocking that Szymon was grinning from ear to ear.

"Oh yes," Szymon said. The bookmaker in Walthamstow would have closed his doors for the day, but Szymon would be there bright and early tomorrow morning. Meanwhile, he retraced his steps to the kitchen. As he expected, Anna was back in her room, having left the hapless Andrzej to wash up.

"Do you think Anna would sell some stuff on eBay for me, no questions asked?"

Andrzej showed no hint of surprise, although it was the first time Szymon had broached the subject. "No problem. You want a quick auction, I suppose. She'll split the price fifty fifty, OK?"

They shook hands on it.

He shook hands with the betting shop manager the next morning, too.

"I've been expecting to see you, Mr Berg," the young man said. He smiled ruefully. "We owe you £118,456. And fifty pence. You're a very, very lucky fellow."

"You said you'd make me rich," Szymon pointed out.

"I said it was possible. It wasn't probable. It wasn't even likely, to be honest. The reason accumulators pay out so much is that the odds are infinitesimally small. Like I said, you're extremely fortunate." He laughed, a shrill sound with a nervous edge to it. "Would you mind if we arranged some publicity about your win, Mr Berg? Some of that luck might rub off onto us then; we'd attract a few more punters in here."

"No publicity," Szymon said hastily. He wanted to collect the cash and vanish, before anyone began asking questions about Florian Berg, Boris Brooks or a group of Poles who had been carousing near Oxford Street 36 hours before.

His first act on leaving the betting shop was to call his wife.

"Marta," he said, hoping his voice did not betray his tension. He was both panicky and excited, prepared to speak quickly before she gave him an earful of abuse and switched off her phone. "I have enough money to buy a big flat in Warsaw. Maybe even a house. I've missed you and Tomasz so much. Can we all live together again, back home?"

He listened patiently as she articulated her disbelief.

"I had savings," he lied. "You never asked me; you just left without a word."

It was still not an easy conversation. She wanted to know why he'd said nothing before. What, she demanded, had he been doing with his money since she left London? Szymon found himself promising to transfer funds to her bank account the next day.

At last, her hectoring tone changed. A smile slowly crept across Szymon's face. To the surprise of shoppers nearby, he punched the air. After that, he found a travel agent and booked his flight home.

Chapter 38 Andrew's first day

Monday morning dawned with birdsong and bright sunlight. Awake even earlier than usual, Andrew had a quick dip in his pool, then chose a designer suit for his first day at GardNet. He wanted his new team to know he meant business. Lingering only long enough for his coffee to cool, he hit the road by six o'clock. He couldn't afford to waste time. GardNet hadn't signed the lease on its new office in Birmingham yet, so he was driving to its plush premises in the City of London.

With such an early start, he missed the Birmingham rush hour, but there was no avoiding it in London. Unlike Shoreditch, he was in the congestion charge zone too. He made a mental note to ask his PA to settle the fee later, amazed that Londoners paid for the privilege of driving through the capital yet still the roads and Tube trains were full. Just like any kind of personal space, parking was in short supply. He appreciated his good fortune that the secure garage underneath the office had a slot reserved for GardNet.

Andrew was seated at his new desk just before nine. He observed that his office, formerly Jed's of course, was extraordinarily spacious. This was in stark contrast to the small cubicles occupied by his colleagues, assuming they were lucky enough to avoid the even more cramped open plan area. At least the fruit, sweets and mineral water were still in evidence. There was no point making any changes now. With luck, he would collect the keys in Birmingham this week, and could move in by the end of the month.

He introduced himself to Valerie when she arrived half an hour later, made a few phone calls and then asked to see Mark.

"I'm delighted you've decided to stay with GardNet," he told the CFO. "I'd like to agree with you our priorities for the next six months. After that, I've asked Val to gather everyone together at eleven, and we'll make an announcement."

"I've put some cost reduction measures in place," Mark said. "We've just exchanged contracts to sell the flat in St Pancras at a huge profit, so that'll shrink the overdraft."

"Good. We'll save even more by moving to Birmingham. I understand from Lucy that all employees have been briefed and she has arranged relocation assistance."

"You've been talking to the HR bunny?"

Andrew raised an eyebrow. "Is that what you call her?" It was rather pejorative. He suspected the nickname said more about Mark than Lucy. "She seems perfectly efficient to me. Let's decide what else we tell our colleagues later, then we'll run it past her as well. I don't just want to talk about cost-cutting. There's a success story to communicate too. GardNet is growing."

"The South Shields call centre has attracted a lot of business, it's true," Mark said.

"And that's not all," Andrew said. "Although GardNet has a datacentre in Docklands already, Stargate is prepared to invest cash in building more. Some of our clients have back offices in the provinces, in Leeds and Birmingham to name but two. With local datacentres and helpdesks, we can give a better service and they'll pay us more."

"Really?" Mark sounded dubious.

"I made a point of meeting several of GardNet's biggest clients last month," Andrew said. "They told me they wanted first line support face to face as well as over the phone. Accordingly, I asked Stargate to make the resources available."

"Jed would never have done that."

"No. This company will be run very differently in future."

The announcement was made in Andrew's office. He suspected most of the GardNet staff had never visited it before. "I'm Andrew Aycliffe," he began. "It's my pleasure to meet you all today. I've got great plans for GardNet and I want to share them with you.

This company is getting bigger. We're bringing more jobs to Britain, and more jobs near our customers. That means not just in London. And that brings me to a key point: I want you guys to have a work-life balance. Holidays when you want them. Homeworking. No more long commutes. We're moving the head office to Birmingham, as you already know. It's a city well known for culture and sport, especially football," he looked around, saw a few suppressed chuckles, and added, "several teams in fact, of which the best plays at Villa Park, but I'm a realist – I know you don't all agree. More importantly, the average travel to work time is less than thirty minutes. I hope as many of you as possible will decide to join me at our new offices near the cathedral. Do you have any questions?"

As if on cue, his iPhone rang. He saw it was Melissa. "I'll take that question later," he joked, switching the phone to its silent mode.

Lucy spoke up. "Would you like me to outline the new flexible benefits package, Andrew?"

"Yes please," he said gratefully. He really liked her: bright, positive and with plenty of ideas that could flourish now Jed Gardner was no longer pouring cold water on them. He'd given Mark the task of persuading her to move from London. Mark's charm had every chance of succeeding, assuming, Andrew reflected, that the CFO never revealed to Lucy the nickname he was using for her.

He discovered Lucy had brought a laptop, projector and PowerPoint presentation. She spent five minutes breezing through it. Andrew barely listened, wondering why Melissa was calling him at work. He let Lucy field most of the questions. He was quite touched to see her glow with pride at the opportunity.

To Andrew's relief, news of the move was generally well-received. "Come back at one o'clock and I'll have some beers in for you," he told everyone. Alone again, he called Melissa.

"I've just had some awful news," she said. "The police phoned. Boris has been found dead."

Andrew reeled. Once the initial shock had passed, he was curious to know more. Boris, and a huge slug of GardNet's money, had been missing for months. If the police knew the whereabouts of one, they might yet find the other. The thought crossed his mind that a phone call to the police might be productive. Before delving into Boris' fate, though, he wanted to be sure Melissa was all right. "How do you feel?" he asked.

"Shaken," Melissa admitted. "Boris was the biggest mistake of my life, but he didn't deserve to die like that."

"What do you mean? How did it happen?"

"They don't know yet, but they think from crushing. His body was discovered in a dustcart which had collected refuse from the West End." Melissa's voice trembled. "The police are pretty sure he was still alive when he ended up in the garbage truck. I can't bear to think of it. He must have seen its steel jaws, must have known what was about to happen. I can't understand why he didn't scream, why no one rescued him."

"He was probably asleep," Andrew said, hoping to console her. "He wouldn't have known anything about it." Even to his own ears, he sounded unconvincing. It was equally likely that Boris had screamed unheard, his voice drowned by the noise of the truck. The refuse collectors wouldn't have been listening for him. No one would anticipate any living creature bigger than a rat to be subsisting among the waste.

"I do hope so. But Andrew, I feel desperately sorry for him. To be reduced to living in a waste bin – what could have happened to Boris since he disappeared? Do you think it was suicide?"

Andrew immediately discounted that possibility. £80m in liquid assets would give anyone a reason to live. "It must have been a sad accident," he said. While he didn't want to give her false hope, he felt obliged to ask, "Are the police completely sure it's Boris they've found?" He suspected it would be hard to identify anyone mangled to a pulp in a dustcart.

"They've run DNA and fingerprint tests," Melissa said. "There was a silly misunderstanding a few years ago, when he was caught smoking weed. He accepted a caution for that, so his details were on the police database."

A small mercy, then, that she wouldn't be required to identify the body. Still, it was obvious she needed his support. Andrew wasn't prepared to leave work early on his first day at GardNet, however. He offered a compromise. "Let me see you tonight. I'll be at the club until Friday. In fact, you could stay there all week as my guest if you want to avoid the press. Cancel your appointments, go there now, and lie low. I'll call them now to make sure they're expecting you."

He confessed to himself that he had an ulterior motive. GardNet had never publicly admitted to being a victim of fraud. Even Melissa had no idea that Boris was a thief. The last thing Andrew needed was a media investigation into Boris' death. By removing the most photogenic player in the drama, he would avoid the press whipping themselves to fever pitch over pictures of a pretty woman.

Thankfully, Melissa agreed. Having phoned his club, Andrew called the Fraud Squad. Were they aware that a crime suspect had been found dead? They were very much aware, it transpired, and gave Andrew even more details. While Boris's body had been comprehensively crushed, the contents of his pockets were intact. No wallet had been found, and they were treating this as a clear indication of crime. A hotel key card had been obtained from the corpse, however, and this had resulted in a promising lead to the missing millions.

Andrew shuddered. The binmen who discovered the body at their depot had, apparently, vomited at the sight of it and were still on sick leave. Andrew was glad he had promised beers all round at lunchtime, feeling suddenly in need of Dutch courage himself.

"Planning to do any work this afternoon?" Mark asked, as Andrew downed three beers in quick succession in front of his colleagues.

Andrew hinted at the news.

"Oh, that," Mark said dismissively. "I already saw it in the Bloomberg newsfeed. He got what he deserved, in my opinion."

"Did they insinuate Boris was a crook?" Andrew asked.

"Not at all," Mark said. "The GardNet Triangle got another mention, though."

Andrew was about to open another beer when Valerie said there was a caller on the line.

"Who is it?"

"She won't say," Valerie replied. "In the circumstances, I wouldn't usually put a call through to you, but she says £100,000 is at stake."

"Can you put her through to Mark?"

"I've tried that. She's refusing to talk to anyone but you. I thought, with a sum of money like that..."

"OK, I'll take it," Andrew said. Valerie seemed sensible enough, although after only a morning at GardNet, it was impossible to know for sure.

"Hello, Mr Aycliffe," the caller said. "I'm Diani Potter."

"Dee Arnie?"

"Yes, Diani. I'm named after a tropical holiday paradise."

He didn't know of it, and was immediately sceptical. "How can I help you, Miss Potter?" he asked. "I can only spare two minutes for you, I'm afraid."

"It's Mrs," Diani said. "I've been meaning to tell someone."

She sounded nervous. Andrew imagined her wringing her hands. "Yes?" he asked.

"About three months ago, I received £100,000 in my bank account."

"Congratulations. Why are you telling me?"

"Because you're the new boss at GardNet, and I think the cash might be yours."

Andrew almost dropped the phone. "Talk me through it, Diani." It really was a ridiculous name, and he couldn't help grinning.

"I'm a widow. My husband died of alcohol poisoning at Boris Brooks' wedding."

He dimly recalled Melissa alluding to the death as proof that her marriage had been doomed from the beginning. "I'm sorry to hear that," he said.

"Thank you. It isn't easy with six small children."

For once, Andrew did not know what to say. "I should think not," he mumbled. He felt desperately sorry for her. "Carry on," he added.

"I hear Boris Brooks is dead too, possibly murdered," Diani said. "He disappeared when my bank account was miraculously boosted, and I believe, at around the time your company had financial difficulties."

"What makes you say that?" Andrew asked, trying to make his voice sound casual.

"Why else would Jed Gardner leave suddenly, carrying a bin liner?"

She was surprisingly insightful. Andrew's mind raced. If Brooks really had arranged a transfer of cash to Diani, out of guilt, sympathy, desire or some other reason, then her bank might be able to say where the funds had originated. That in turn could help him discover where the rest had gone, assuming Boris' killers hadn't already absconded with it.

"You need to talk to the police," he said finally. "One last thing, Diani. You have my word that GardNet will not try to recover the money from you. Keep it. Give me your address, and I'll make sure you get that message in writing."

Her painful honesty deserved a reward, he felt. She need never have told him, or anyone else, about her windfall. Someone like her, a widow with six other mouths to feed, needed £100,000. Stargate, Danville and Ross could manage without it. Anyway, with her help, he was a lot closer to recovering a far greater sum for GardNet.

"Are you sure?" Diani asked.

"If anyone doesn't like it, they can hold me accountable," Andrew replied. He could handle Angie Ross and her unsmiling eyes.

Chapter 39 Lianne's rescuer

The morning's session with Mark had gone well. He had mentioned that his job was moving to Birmingham, which saved Lianne the trouble of telling him not to return. She was bored with her clients and the pointlessness of her work. In her mind, her suitcase was already packed.

While Mark showered, Lianne began checking emails. Her schedule was busy for the rest of the day: lunch with Andrew, then afternoon tea with Caz to make plans for Kenya.

Mark's phone was constantly ringing, disturbing her concentration. She fished around for it in his jacket pocket.

"What are you doing?" Mark was emerging into the lobby from the bathroom, his face like thunder. "You're spying on me, aren't you?"

Lianne stood her ground. "How dare you speak to me like that. You're lucky I haven't stamped on your phone with my stilettos. It's as annoying as you are. Take it with you, worm, and don't bother coming back."

She was unprepared for his response.

"Callous bitch," Mark said. "You've been playing with me for too long, Lianne." To her shock, he lunged at her.

Lianne was wearing an extremely short, tight black dress with a full-length zip at the front. She'd intended to change it before leaving to see Andrew. Mark tugged on the zip, exposing her bra. He clawed at her breasts. At the same time, he pressed his face into hers, forcing her lips open with his tongue.

Lianne struggled. Although she was extremely fit, Mark had weight on his side, not to mention the element of surprise. She tried to scream, but her teeth rendered the sound inaudible, clamped shut as they were against Mark's insistent tongue. At last, she pushed a hand under his bulk and grabbed the fleshy parts of his groin, squeezing hard.

Mark's reaction was far slower and more deliberate than she expected. Instead of jerking backwards, he moved both hands to Lianne's throat.

He must have a very high pain threshold, she realised belatedly as she gasped for breath. She began to see stars. Her head throbbed and her heart pounded. He increased the compression until she no longer had the strength to grip him.

As her consciousness slipped away, Lianne heard her doorbell, a distant sound, like a dream. The hold on her throat did not relax. Again, even softer, she heard the bell, usually so strident. There was a faint rattle. Then Mark's voice was saying, "He's going to break down the door. You'd better answer it."

Roughly, he pulled away from her. Lianne gulped air into her lungs: huge, grateful, greedy breaths. She staggered to her feet, zipping up her dress.

She was standing right next to the front door, and could see a figure through its rippled glass: a man who was hammering with his fists so hard that the panes shook in their frame. "Open up," he demanded. She recognised Andrew's voice.

There was a glittery evening shawl hanging in the lobby. Lianne had the presence of mind to fling the garment around her neck before opening the door.

"Come in," Lianne said, her unforeseen deliverance bringing her to tears. She ushered Andrew across the threshold.

She watched as his eyes narrowed. Mark, meanwhile, was gawping at his boss. Had the last ten minutes not taken place, Lianne would have been amused at the look on Mark's face. Perhaps he was speculating whether she knew Andrew professionally. He would almost certainly be aware now that his suspicions about her were correct. Despite the summer heat wafting through the open doorway, she shivered.

"We've just finished our session," she said as perkily as she could, hoping Andrew wouldn't notice the tension in her voice. "Mark was saying how excited he is to be moving to Birmingham." She could still feel her heart pounding.

"Indeed," Mark muttered. "I can't wait." He wouldn't meet her eyes, or Andrew's. "I'd better be on my way, then. Heaps to do this afternoon."

As the door slammed behind Mark, Andrew turned to Lianne. "What was all that about?"

"I don't know what you mean," Lianne said. "Shouldn't I be the one asking questions? We were supposed to see each other at your club."

"I texted you an hour ago," Andrew said. "My meeting finished early. The weather's so fine, I thought you might like to visit that gastropub in Belsize Park you told me about." His face darkened. "You mentioned you'd be in a rush, so I thought I'd drive over to you. I can't say I was expecting this. Are you having an affair with Mark?"

"No."

She'd resolved to say as little as possible, but Andrew wouldn't drop the subject.

159

"Lianne, you were as close as this." He hooked both his index fingers together.

By way of reply, Lianne removed the shawl, revealing the imprint of her assailant's fingers upon her neck.

Andrew gasped. It was clear he understood all too well. "Just wait until I see Mark again," he said grimly. "I'll thump him so hard, he'll land in the next county. As for his job – he can forget it." His voice softened. "Lianne, are you OK? Do you want me to take you to a police station?"

"No," Lianne said. She couldn't imagine a pleasant time explaining her business to the local constabulary. "And I don't want you to hit Mark either, or fire him; at least, not unless you're sure you don't need him."

"As you say, then," Andrew agreed. "I'd like Mark to help me move GardNet's office to Birmingham, but once that's done, he'll be out on his ear." He added ruefully, "I'd started to wonder about his attitude to women, and you've confirmed my fears."

Lianne was still feeling subdued. "Andrew, I'd rather not go out. I'll cook lunch here."

"You're kidding," Andrew said. "I drove all this way to show you my car, and you won't let me?" He grinned.

"All right," Lianne acquiesced. He was obviously trying to lift her spirits. She said, "I guess my cooking's too healthy for you?" and was rewarded with a wink.

Andrew's red sports car was around the corner. "You like my little baby?" he asked. "Sleek and smooth, isn't she? Quick too. I'll show you – as much as London traffic allows me to."

"I won't talk," Lianne said. "You concentrate on driving." Gradually, she recovered her equilibrium as he whizzed through the city streets.

"What news?" Andrew asked, once they were seated in the pub garden, menus and drinks before them. This time, Andrew had insisted on beer for him and Pimms for her.

"I've made up my mind," Lianne said, raising her glass of Pimms. "I'm going to Kenya with Caz. She asked me to thank you for the very generous donation. She thinks it's enough for a school, a workshop, a farm and all sorts of activities."

"Did I send her any cash?" Andrew asked, hitting his forehead. "I'm sure I remember forgetting."

"She's convinced she received it." Caz had intimated that it was a substantial sum of money. If it was of so little consequence to Andrew, he must be even wealthier than she'd thought.

"She's welcome, then," Andrew said. "How long will you stay in Kenya?"

"Maybe forever," Lianne teased him. Seeing his crestfallen face, she said, "Six to twelve months. But I don't suppose we'll see each other much when I come back to London. GardNet is upping sticks to Birmingham, after all."

"It was a condition of my accepting the job," Andrew said. "I don't want to live in London again. I've been there, got the T shirt."

"How did your guys at GardNet react when you told them?"

"Very well, actually," Andrew said. "They really get it. They know they'll have a better quality of life when we've moved. I'm still arranging for training in change management to anyone who wants it. I'd planned to ask if you'd run a workshop, but I don't suppose you will after what happened today. You'll hardly want to see Mark Trelawney again."

"Of course I'll do it," Lianne said, her confidence restored by Pimms. "I'm not scared of him." She would simply be on her guard with Mark. He would never have the opportunity to surprise her again, even if he turned up at her flat. She was about to rent it to an ex-Army martial arts instructor, anyway. Inwardly, she gloated, visualising Mark's expression when she arrived at his office to deliver the workshop. That alone would make it worthwhile, quite apart from the considerable fee she would charge.

"You've done change management training before, I take it?"

"Yes," Lianne lied, unfazed by her lack of experience. She would research the subject, perhaps read a couple of management books, and rely on her usual chutzpah to win the day.

"Anyway," Andrew said, "I've got some really exciting news. I'm going to pop the question to Melissa."

"That's sudden. You've been together for how long? Four months?"

"Yes," Andrew said. "Long enough to know I've found the mother of my children."

"Hold on," Lianne said. "Isn't she a respected musician, with a base here? I mean, she set up the Orchestra of London. There's a clue in that name. She won't want to follow you to Birmingham like Mark Trelawney and the geeks at GardNet."

161

"She makes virtually no money out of that orchestra. Unlike you, Melissa can't even afford her own flat," Andrew said. "She should be happy to give up all that musical stuff. Anyway, she really wants a family. That's why she proposed to Boris Brooks."

"And look how that ended," Lianne said.

"Yes, she's had it rough," Andrew said. "His funeral was a bad day for her, to put it mildly."

"You went with her, I suppose?"

"No. Too much work." He glimpsed Lianne's outraged expression, and protested, "I didn't even know the man. And it's not as if Jed Gardner was going to be there, to make the situation even more difficult for her. He hated Brooks. In fact, he was a murder suspect for a while, but the police ruled him out. Computer records proved he hadn't been in London for weeks, apparently." His face brightened. "I'm as sure as I can be that Melissa is the right woman for me. We've even talked about children's names."

Only a few months ago, he'd seemed certain Lianne could be the right woman for him, if only she would accept his workaholic ways. She thanked her lucky stars that she'd resisted rekindling their old romance. Cheekily, she said, "These children whose names you've chosen. Will you be leaving your office at five to see them each evening?"

He looked horrified. "Of course not. Someone's got to bring home the bacon. Anyway, Melissa won't want me interfering in her domain."

"You don't want a life partner," Lianne said. "You want a brood mare."

"Melissa's not like you. She wants babies. What's wrong with that?" Andrew persisted.

Lianne looked away, imagining Melissa like a royal princess in a tower, alone while her Prince Charming spent a hundred hours a week in the corporate world. Did she really know what Andrew was planning?

Chapter 40 Jed alone

Jed parked his bicycle by the front door at Cherry Trees, and pressed the bell. He was ushered into the residents' lounge. Unlike his time at GardNet, when Eleanor was lucky to receive a visit every couple of months, he was now able to see her almost every day. Cherry Trees was not far from the cottage. On his old bicycle, gleaming with new paint, oil and polish, he could travel there in minutes.

"I brought the Times," he said to her. "I thought we could do the crossword." It appeared that crossword puzzles warded off dementia, and Jed cherished a dream that Eleanor would regain her sharp mind one day. She could still solve a few of the clues by herself. With his help, they usually completed the puzzle and moved on to Sudoku.

Jed never usually bought a newspaper, preferring to keep up to date online, but he invested in the Times for Eleanor's sake. He bought his own copy rather than obliging Cherry Trees to order it for her. Without his chivvying, she would never look at it. He had noticed, too, that the nurses were less than pleased to find a completed crossword in one of the newspapers available in the lounge.

"Shall we look at the wedding announcements, Gerald?" Eleanor said "I like to see if my friends are getting married."

That was how he saw Melissa and Aycliffe were engaged. Jed recoiled, dropping the flimsy paper. He should have expected this. Aycliffe seemed determined to take everything that Jed held dear. Eleanor alone was left to him.

She squeezed his hand, her eyes twinkling. "You don't look well, Gerald. Would you like to lie down in your room? I'll bring you a tonic."

In spite of his bitter disappointment, Jed smiled at the notion. He knew she did not mean a G&T. Throughout his childhood, Eleanor had been a firm believer in the restorative powers of branded energy drinks. Jed, too, had fallen under the same spell until the day he idly read the ingredients list printed on the bottle she had handed him. He now appreciated it was simply fizzy water with sugar and caffeine, and no more a magic potion than a cup of tea. That, of course, was Eleanor's other answer to life's woes.

"No thanks," he said. "Let's finish the crossword."

He left at five, cycling to the cottage and preparing himself for an evening in the garden. The luxuriant weeds he had found there, the result of two years' unchecked growth, were now almost vanquished. Better still, he was discovering tougher varieties of fruit and vegetables as they emerged from the green stranglehold: strawberries, potatoes, onions, rhubarb.

It was just as well, because Jed had resolved to be careful with money. He had substantial savings, but he was not earning an income, and Cherry Trees was costly. With care, Jed believed he could fund Eleanor's stay there for ten years before he had to work again.

He missed that work, though. The cottage, all dust banished, and the tamed garden were poor substitutes for the elegance of computer algorithms. With the broadband he had installed at the cottage, he still went online and, anonymously, solved IT problems posted by other geeks. He wouldn't have claimed he was happy, but his existence had bright spots: his secret life online, the physical satisfaction of gardening, his quiet times with Eleanor.

He was getting over GardNet.

The light was fading and he was just cleaning his tools when Jed heard the phone. Dashing inside, he knew he wouldn't reach it in time.

He checked the number of the missed call. It was Cherry Trees, he was sure. They wouldn't phone, especially at this hour, unless they had bad news. Trembling, Jed rang them back.

"Mr Gardner? I'm afraid your mother has been taken ill," the nurse said. "She's unconscious. We suspect a stroke."

Jed wanted to rail at her that a medical professional should know if it was a stroke, not merely have an idea that it might be. Instead, wanting to keep Eleanor's carers onside, he forced himself to be civil. "Have you called a doctor?" he asked.

"I called an ambulance. She's being admitted to the RUH. Their visiting times are over for the day, I think, but you're welcome to see her there tomorrow morning. I assume your work allows that? I would go if I were you."

"Yes," Jed said, "my work allows that." His bicycle was adequate to the task too. The Royal United Hospital in Bath was under ten miles away. After the call, it occurred to him that Virginia should be told that her sister was unwell. He immediately phoned her.

"I'll ring the hospital to see how she is, dear," Virginia said, as Jed wished he'd thought of doing so himself.

His aunt called him back a few minutes later to tell him that Eleanor appeared to be recovering well, and they should visit the next morning. Although Virginia lived in Bath, she insisted she would drive to the cottage to collect Jed. On arrival at the hospital, however, they discovered they were too late. Eleanor had just suffered another massive stroke. She was dead.

Chapter 41 Lianne takes a risk

Lianne made a note of everything she had to do before flying to Kenya with Caz. Find a tenant, have injections, buy new clothes, dump boyfriend, phone clients, ring Melissa. It was only the last that was problematic. She rather despised her clients, and she was rapidly reaching her boredom threshold with her latest boyfriend. Ringing Melissa, however, meant risking her friendship with Andrew.

It was that very friendship that gave Lianne the resolve to act, however. Andrew's impending marriage was a disaster waiting to happen. If Lianne did nothing, he would be divorcing within five years.

Finding Melissa's number wasn't easy. Lianne first telephoned the Orchestra of London's box office, guessing a member of the orchestra would be manning it. She was right, but ended up speaking to a cello player who wouldn't divulge Melissa's contact details. She searched online in vain. Finally, she called in a complicated series of favours through a client who directed musicals.

Having prepared what she was going to say, Lianne made the call at five in the afternoon. By then, Melissa's tutoring would be done for the day, she would not be playing for an audience, and there was no way Andrew would have left work yet to be with her.

"Good evening, Melissa. I'm Lianne, an old friend of Andrew's. We met at the Orangery," Lianne said.

"I remember. His ex-girlfriend. You're top of our wedding invitation list." Melissa didn't sound unduly concerned.

"I've known Andrew for a long time," Lianne said. "We split up because of his workaholism, actually. From what I've seen, he hasn't changed."

Melissa laughed. "I need to train him, then."

"I'm not sure anyone can. Andrew will always put himself, and his work, first. He expects you to give up your music and be the little wifey, keeping the home fires burning and popping out children for him."

There was a pause before Melissa said, "How do you know?"

"He told me," Lianne said simply. "Also, I've known Andrew for years. He's a Villa fan, not a music man." She added, "Isn't it too soon to be marrying, on the rebound from two failed relationships?"

"Two?" Melissa said, annoyance creeping into her voice. "There was no relationship with Jed Gardner, whatever the gossip columns said."

"When they said he left work early to be with you, was that wrong too? Jed Gardner was wedded to his work just as much as Andrew. In fact, if any man in your life has been prepared to compromise for you, it's Jed Gardner."

Again, Melissa was silent, this time for longer. Lianne wondered if she'd ended the call, but looking at her phone, she could see it was still open. "Listen, it's better to think about this now than when you're stuck in an unhappy marriage far away from your friends," Lianne pleaded.

"I don't know why you called me. Are you really so over Andrew yourself?" Melissa asked.

Melissa was trying to hit the jugular, Lianne thought, sighing. Although she liked Andrew a great deal, she was scarcely blind to his selfishness. He was attracted to strong women, but would make no concessions to their desires. "If we're discussing motives," Lianne said, "ask yourself whether revenge on Jed Gardner might be driving Andrew in any way."

Melissa gasped. "I'll do better than that. I'll ask Andrew."

"You should," Lianne agreed.

Chapter 42 Jed's farewell

"Can you cope alone, Jed?" Virginia asked. They were returning to her car, parked a short distance from the hospital. "You can stay with me in Bath for a few days if you like."

"I'd rather be at the cottage," Jed said, adding quickly, "but do you think you could arrange the funeral?" He recalled Eleanor having to do this for one of her brothers, and saying it was extraordinarily complicated. Selecting an undertaker, venue, clothes for the deceased, flowers, a suitable wake – there were so many choices, all apparently charged with significance for family, friends and neighbours. Despite offering sympathy at the time, Jed had pleaded pressure of work rather than attend his uncle's funeral. He wished he could avoid Eleanor's, in fact. He shuddered at the thought of a large gathering of strangers and half-remembered acquaintances.

"Of course, dear," Virginia said. "Come back with me for a cup of tea before we return to the cottage."

He preferred a night-dark espresso, and she happily obliged, pressing on him a slab of home-made fruit cake.

"Why don't you take the rest of the cake home for your visitors?" she suggested.

He protested that no guests were expected, but she was insistent. On his return to the cottage, he discovered she was right. So many neighbours visited to offer condolences and advice, he was rarely alone. He made hot drinks, offered cake and said little, nodding his head as he listened to platitudes about Eleanor. What a diamond she was, the salt of the earth, and a sad loss to village life. It momentarily crossed his mind that he had never seen any of these folk visiting her at Cherry Trees.

"I expect that's a coincidence," Virginia said, seeing the positive in everyone as usual. She was sitting in the poky front room of the cottage, a far cry from the Georgian townhouse she shared with her husband in Bath. "I just want to tell you what I've got planned for the funeral, dear."

"I really don't mind," Jed muttered. "You do whatever you want."

"She asked for a Quaker ceremony," Virginia said. "It's stipulated in her will. That means the Friends' Meeting House in Bath rather than the village church."

"Eleanor's dead," Jed said. "I don't suppose she'll either know or care."

"We should respect her beliefs," Virginia said. "I've booked the Friends' Meeting House for Thursday afternoon at three o'clock, and then we'll have a wake at your village hall so your local friends can go."

"Her local friends," Jed pointed out.

Virginia smoothed over the graceless remark. "Yes, dear. The Women's Institute and the Friends of the Earth and all the other little groups Eleanor supported."

Through Virginia's efforts, announcements appeared in the local newspapers and on noticeboards in the village. Jed looked forward to Thursday with apprehension. Virginia had opted for a silent funeral, which meant no one had to speak unless they wanted to. She had, however, told him she hoped he would say a few words about his adoptive mother.

On the day itself, Jed awoke late after a restless night of muddled nightmares and dark reflections on the finality of death. During Eleanor's time at Cherry Trees, he had treasured dreams of a cure for Alzheimer's, a magic bullet that would restore her faculties and permit her to return home. Now, she would never see the cottage again. With a degree of trepidation, he cycled to Bath. Although it was hardly a metropolis like London, he was already starting to feel uncomfortable among the crowds there. It was high summer now, bringing hordes of tourists to exclaim at the town's beauty. He left his bicycle chained to railings outside the Friends' Meeting House, in clear contravention of a notice exhorting him not to do so.

Jed rather admired the two hundred-year-old building, which he had visited many times in his youth. He assumed it was a Roman temple as imagined by its Georgian builders. Entering the door past its imposing columns, he was assailed by a familiar and thankful sense of tranquillity.

Although he was twenty minutes early, Virginia and her family were already waiting inside to greet guests. While the menfolk wore suits, Virginia and her daughter were dressed in colourful summer frocks.

"Jed, we'll have to hide that jacket," Virginia exclaimed, smoothly removing his high-visibility jerkin and stuffing it into her capacious handbag.

Jed was amazed. "Why?" It was a fluorescent yellow. Surely that was in keeping with the Quaker philosophy of wearing bright colours to celebrate the life of the deceased?

169

"It's a bit scruffy, dear," Virginia said. "That blue shirt and jeans are too, but they'll have to do. Have you got your speech written out, by the way?"

"Yes." It really was only a few words, and he had practiced in front of his mirror until he was confident he wouldn't stumble over them.

"Well done. Monica, why don't you take Jed through to the meeting room and find somewhere comfortable to sit?"

His cousin ushered him to the floor above. "This is the largest room," she explained. "Aunt Eleanor had a lot of friends."

He wasn't sure if Monica expected an answer, and he remained silent, anxiously inspecting the rows of empty seats and imagining them full. He shuddered. Now he had spent so long in business, the layout of the room reminded Jed of a rather downmarket conference: serried ranks of wood-framed chairs with blue cushions. The coffin, placed in the centre of the room, was the only clue that an army of accountants and lawyers were not about to arrive. It was bedecked with bows and ribbons of all hues, flowers and photographs.

"Mum wanted it to be pretty," Monica said, following his eyes. "Aunt Eleanor asked for biodegradable cardboard, so we jazzed it up a bit."

Jed nodded. "Thank you."

"Sit at the front, Jed," Monica suggested. "Unless you're afraid of ghosts, and anyway, Aunt Eleanor would be the friendliest sort of phantom, I'm sure."

Jed waved the comment away. "I don't believe in ghosts." He was not superstitious in the slightest.

"I'll stay here with you," Monica said. "We'll save a seat for Mum."

They sat together, silently. Gradually, other mourners filtered into the room, many of them dressed in black despite clear instructions on Virginia's invitations. The room remained quiet.

Jed fidgeted, and glanced at his smartphone. It was two minutes to three, and the room was almost full. He desperately wished the ceremony, and the day, was over.

Virginia was standing by the door. Apparently satisfied that all the funeral guests had arrived, she closed it and took centre stage. A vision in bright red and white polka dots, his aunt easily commanded the mourners' attention.

"Good afternoon, everyone, and welcome," she said. "Thank you for coming to celebrate the life of my dear sister, Eleanor." She gestured to the gaudily decorated coffin at her feet. "Eleanor was a Quaker, as I am myself, and as are many of us here. Our belief as Quakers is that the light of God resides in each and every one of us, and today all of us bring happy memories of Eleanor and the light she shone on our lives. This ceremony is a silent one, which means we will sit quietly until the spirit moves us to speak. I am sure many of us will wish to say a few words about Eleanor." She glanced at Jed. "Feel free to speak when you will." She sat in the empty chair next to him, and squeezed his hand.

The format of the ceremony was familiar to Jed. He enjoyed the stillness that followed; the illusion of solitude within a crowd. Eventually, Virginia herself broke the silence to say that Eleanor had been the best elder sister and role model a girl could have. Eleanor's cup overflowed with happiness for all of her life. Her sister's one regret was that she never married, but even this did not stop her experiencing the unique joy brought by a child, as Eleanor had adopted little Gerald, and look how handsome and intelligent he was now.

Jed blushed. The eyes of the whole congregation were upon him. He should deliver his eulogy now, allowing the spotlight to pass swiftly elsewhere. He rose to his feet, reaching in his pocket for the notebook in which a few sentences were neatly written.

"Eleanor Gardner adopted me when I was five years old," he began. The door opened.

If the latecomer had hoped she would slip into the room unnoticed, she had been mistaken. The rest of the assembly might be focusing on Jed, but he saw only Melissa. Like a shining angel, she stood frozen in his gaze. A shaft of sunlight blazed upon her, bleaching her pale hair and white dress still further.

He gasped in shock, the book falling from his hand. Without it, he was lost for words, but only for a moment. Unaccountably, he found he could express his feelings with ease. Fluent language flowed in a torrent, as he ignored his prepared remarks and spoke from his heart.

"She was the first person to show me love," he said. "Maybe I was – am – hard to love, almost unlovable, one might say. Yet Eleanor found it possible." He paused, fighting back the tears that threatened to fall. "To me, she was more than a mother. She was my guardian, my protector. Rather than simply give birth to me, she chose me and fought the law to keep me. Every parent is a special person but I'd say some are more special than others. Eleanor took a child the orphanage considered an untameable beast, and she showed me how to be someone she could be proud of."

Still, Melissa stayed motionless at the entrance to the chamber. Jed addressed his oration solely to her. "You may have known me as an adult, when I had carved a career in the world. I've made mistakes then, but they were nothing compared with my early life. Eleanor had to teach me how to speak, to listen to others, and to understand what others expected of me – and perhaps what I could expect from others. I still can't read people." He spoke without self-pity. He was simply saying it the way it was. "But that's expected of geeks, isn't it? Luckily, Eleanor spotted my talent for IT and encouraged it. I was successful," he looked around now, "at least, for a long while."

She was still there, staying to listen. Their eyes met briefly before she looked away. Hope rose in his heart, and he immediately batted it away. She was engaged to Aycliffe, and anyway, what right did he have to be distracted from his grief at his guardian's passing? "Eleanor was my touchstone," he said. "Our planet is a darker place without her. I loved her, yet she has left my world."

His bereavement was too raw now; his confusion at Melissa's presence overwhelming him further. Jed couldn't contain his tears any longer. "I'm sorry," he sobbed, "I can't carry on." He staggered to his seat.

Virginia passed him a tissue. He could see she wished to hug him and he deliberately turned away, totally overwhelmed by his memories: of Eleanor championing him, of Melissa playing the flute, and then his awful awakening to Melissa's treachery and Eleanor's death. For the rest of the funeral, Jed sat with his head in his hands, hardly noticing when anyone else spoke. Melissa had found one of the few remaining chairs and struck a pose of contemplation, her hands clasped. Why was she here? He occasionally sneaked a glance at her, but her body language was a closed book to him.

Finally, Virginia concluded the service with a prayer written by William Penn. Jed had heard the familiar verse many times before; Quakers often said it in memory of the dead. As Virginia intoned, "Death is no more than a turning of us over from time to eternity," his thoughts drifted from the past back to the present. He could not leave the chamber without passing Melissa. Like a shipwrecked sailor clinging to flotsam, he longed to hold her in his arms. Horrified at his lack of reason, he told himself to avoid her. She was promised to another man, and, worse, Jed had nothing to say to her. All of his vocabulary, his short-lived fluency with words, had been spent in his address to the funeral-goers. As the other mourners stretched and left their seats, talking together, Jed alone remained. Refusing eye contact, he hoped Melissa would leave as suddenly as she had appeared, flying on a sunbeam like a pale angel.

She did not. Melissa lingered, waiting until even Virginia, with an uneasy backward glance at Jed, had departed. If he wished to follow his aunt, he would have to confront Melissa too. He rose from his seat, looking at the ground, refusing her eye contact.

"Jed." It was no use. He could not ignore her. Their eyes met. Her expression was one of concern, almost mirroring his. She stood before him, holding out her arms. "I'm sorry," she said.

Awkwardly, Jed let her embrace him. For the first time in his adult life, he was close to a woman, and he was almost overpowered by the sensation: the warmth of Melissa's skin, the light, flowery scent of her hair and the feeling of life that coursed through him. He pulled away from her and stroked her hair, silkier than his own and shining spun gold in the summer light. "Why did you come here?" he asked.

"To see you," she said, adding quickly, "I've left Andrew. He tried to persuade me that you didn't care about me, that you were cold and lacked the capacity for love." She shivered, although there was no chill in the air. "I know it isn't true. No one could hear you speak about your adoptive mother without realising the depth of your affection for her. Andrew was mistaken about that. Worse, for me, Andrew was a mistake. Music means everything to me, and nothing to him. We were wrong for each other, and in the chaos of my split with Boris, I just didn't see that."

At the mention of Boris' name, she fell silent and looked away. Unpractised as he was in divining emotions, Jed sensed that Boris' death must be troubling her. He held out his hands, a clumsy gesture for him, but one that he thought Eleanor would have used.

Melissa took them. "I hope it will be third time lucky," she said. "If you'll still have me, of course."

"What do you think?" he said, finding a smile as his spirits rose again.

She clutched his hands. "I can hope," she said. Then, slowly, she beamed too.

"How did you know I was here?" he asked.

173

"I didn't," Melissa said. "I knew about your cottage; you had some paperwork for it on the table in your London flat. I took a taxi from Bath station to the village. Then I had to ask the driver to come all the way back, when your neighbour told me where you were. It cost me a fortune." She giggled.

It was as if sunshine was dispelling the black fog that had endured within his mind since she had left. Even her laughter was musical, he noticed. "We'll be going to the village again now," he told her. "There's a wake there. I'll see if Virginia can give you a lift."

Outside, however, they found no trace of Virginia and the rest of the congregation. While Jed's bicycle was at their disposal, it wasn't built for two. "Can you cycle?" he asked Melissa. "Because if you can, I'll take the bus and we should arrive at the cottage within half an hour."

The party was to be held in the church hall, but Jed had no intention of going. The attention focused on him at the funeral had been enough. He arrived at the cottage, found Melissa loitering in the garden, and shepherded her inside.

She inspected her surroundings appreciatively, to Jed's relief. The cottage had never seen a makeover from Jeannie or anyone else. It was as it had been when Eleanor lived there: clean, cosy and tidy, but filled with oddly shaped brown furniture and crocheted throws.

"Flagstones, stone walls," Melissa said. "Rather different from London."

"You don't have to live here," Jed blurted out. "Everything you do musically is in London." At once, he regretted saying it. Whatever her news in the meeting house, she might think him presumptuous for imagining they would immediately be living together.

He needn't have feared her reaction. "I can travel there when I need to," Melissa said. "If I'm not mistaken, music happens in Somerset too. Isn't that a piano in the corner?"

"It is," he agreed. "This room has a good acoustic." He and Eleanor had moved rugs and cushions around to achieve it.

"I think I should put that to the test." She began to play a Beethoven piano sonata.

Jed sat cross-legged on the floor at her feet, letting waves of sound submerge him.

She finished with a theatrical flourish. "How was that?"

"Sublime," he said fervently.

174

"I thought so too." Melissa's eyes danced. "What about your passion?" she asked.

Jed reddened, only to find that she was asking about his train set. "I do have one," he admitted, "but it's rather inconveniently situated."

"Show me."

He found his torch, and a ladder, and led her to the attic. There was actually plenty of light within the huge, barn-like room; Eleanor had never insulated it, and there were chinks between all the tiles.

"There," he said proudly. He had built two interconnecting lines, with sidings, stations and a spur servicing an airstrip where a remote-controlled model helicopter waited.

"Can we play?"

"I need my laptop," Jed said. "I have some timetables programmed already." He dashed down the ladder, eager as a ten-year-old to display his toys to their best advantage. At his command, the helicopter buzzed overhead in the tallest part of the room, while trains whizzed in and out of tunnels and stations, sometimes close to each other but never crashing.

"Imagine playing with your children here," Melissa said.

"Yes. I've never had company in the attic before, but I'd enjoy it," Jed said, rather surprising himself. "I have no blood relatives and I think I'd like that too."

He heard a key turn in the lock downstairs, and Virginia shout, "Hello!"

"I'm in the attic," Jed yelled.

"Come down here, then," Virginia said. "You're needed at the party."

He had hoped to stay below the radar of the partygoers, but he knew it was useless to protest now he had been discovered. He descended the ladder, closely followed by Melissa.

Virginia gave her an enquiring look. "I'm Jed's aunt," she said, offering a hand to Melissa.

"Melissa."

"My friend from London," Jed said, although he rather felt that Virginia perceived the explanation as lacking in almost every relevant detail. "I was showing her my train set." Recalling one of the old lady's recent remarks, he added, "Eleanor had suggested it."

"You need to come to the wake, Jed," Virginia said. "Everyone's asking to see you, especially those who are in their cups. As a Quaker, I didn't supply alcohol, but I should have known your villagers better.

They were quite capable of bringing their own. There are two barrels of scrumpy being drained as we speak."

"I should go with you," Melissa said.

"Of course." Jed smiled. His future, which but hours before had stretched into infinite desolation, was suddenly dazzling in its brightness. "Virginia, you go back. I just need to switch off the train set. Five minutes?"

His aunt left, mollified albeit still quizzical. Jed put his arms around Melissa and kissed her tenderly on the lips.

Chapter 43 Andrew seizes the day

Mark bounced into Andrew's office. "It still smells of paint in here," he sniffed. "How are you, mate? I've got some good news."

"Great," Andrew said. "I need some." He made an effort to arrange his features in a smile, although he could barely stand to be near Mark since their encounter at Lianne's flat.

"What's up?"

"Woman trouble." His engagement was over. After asking Melissa icily why she preferred a weirdo like Jed Gardner, he had accepted his ring back, hastily flung at him. He had even allowed her the last word. Better a weirdo than a workaholic, she had said as her parting shot.

"Can't live with them, can't live without them," Mark murmured.

Andrew grimaced. While he was smarting from Melissa's return to his enemy, he realised he didn't really miss her. There was too much work occupying his mind as he snatched GardNet from the jaws of insolvency. His hatred towards Jed Gardner had started to wane before Melissa left, and Andrew no longer wanted to rekindle it. The man had just lost his mother, a single parent. Andrew shuddered, recalling his father's death. He was fortunate that his mother was still there for him. Indeed, with Andrew's emotional and financial support, she had become a rather merry widow.

There would always be another day, another challenge, another chance for Andrew to seize. He resolved to waste no more time thinking about Jed or Melissa, shutting them away in a far corner of his brain, in a locked box he planned never to open.

"Anyway," Andrew said, turning his attention to Mark, "back to business. What's new?"

"Between you and me," Mark said, in a hushed tone conveying matey conspiracy, "the HR bunny likes you. My hot tip for tonight. Get over that bitch with the hair of the dog that bit you."

"I'll bear that in mind," Andrew said drily, wishing Mark were both less familiar towards him and more respectful towards women. At least he wouldn't have to work with the CFO for much longer, although Mark didn't know yet. He added out of curiosity, "What makes you so sure?"

"Trust me," Mark said. "I've seen a lot of her lately, since you made it my mission to lure her to the Midlands."

Andrew thought he detected a predatory expression on Mark's face. "Not too much, I hope. You haven't been playing away?" he asked the CFO.

"No." Mark's reply was swift. "Not in my back yard."

"Glad to hear it," Andrew said, relieved. "Is that gossip all you came to see me about?"

"Of course not," Mark said, his voice rising with excitement. "We've found most of the money Boris stole. Over £79m of it, anyway. It had been through the Bahamas and Cayman Islands, and back to Switzerland."

Andrew whistled. Suddenly, his job had become immeasurably easier. "Sounds like fun," he said. "I wish I'd packed a suitcase and gone with it."

"Although we know where it is, we may not get it back right away," Mark cautioned. "Oh, and Boris burned through just under £1m on his expenses. Of which £100,000 each went to two females: Diani Potter and Caroline Drewitt." He leered. "I hope they were worth it."

Andrew ignored Mark's insinuation. "Diani we already knew about. She was helping us trace the cash, remember? We should let her keep her share as a finder's fee. Caroline Drewitt is another matter."

Her name nagged at Andrew's consciousness. He knew he ought to recognise it. Eventually, he said, "I had an email from her. Caz Drewitt. She's raising funds for an orphanage in Kenya. My ex-girlfriend's flying there with her to build it, actually." He checked the time. "She'll be on a plane there right now."

"Ex-girlfriend?" Mark asked, smirking.

"Not Melissa," Andrew said sharply. There was little point in mentioning Lianne's name to Mark; in fact, recalling Mark's behaviour towards Lianne, he could hardly wait to give the CFO his marching orders.

Lianne had told him that a little money would go a long way in Africa, then congratulated him on his generous donation. Andrew remembered his bewilderment. He was even more sure now that he'd never replied to Caz's email. Evidently, when £100,000 hit her bank account, Caz had believed it was from him. He'd told Lianne he would make a donation, after all.

It was still a mystery why Boris had seen fit to send funds to Caz. Perhaps Mark, with his sniggering innuendo, was right. Andrew sighed.

£100,000 could go a very long way indeed: all the way to a country where, instead of being the price of a fast car, it meant the difference between life and death for a village full of orphans.

"We'll have to ask for it back," Mark said.

Andrew shook his head. "It's gone to a Kenyan orphan charity," he said. "How will that make GardNet look if word leaks out?"

"We can see what Matthew thinks," Mark suggested.

The communications manager couldn't have been more specific. It would be a PR disaster. He urged Andrew and Mark to leave well alone; he, Matthew, could not be responsible for the consequences if GardNet were seen to grab cash from a good cause.

The next milestone would be a conversation with Angie Ross, a dialogue which Andrew had always assumed would revolve around Diani's £100,000 bank receipt. Doubling the stake wouldn't result in a very different discussion. He immediately sent Ross a brief email. Unsurprisingly, he was summoned to Stargate's offices overlooking Tower Bridge. She wanted to meet on home territory. With a wry grin, he walked to the station and bought a ticket to London. She might feel she could intimidate him in her own office. He would prove her wrong.

Angie Ross was noticeably less friendly than at any other time in their brief acquaintance. She kept Andrew waiting for twenty minutes. When he was finally summoned into the glassy box where she controlled Stargate's finances, her expression was stern.

"I'm struggling to understand you," Ross said. "Let me reflect back what I think you're saying. You propose handing over £200,000 of GardNet's money, of Stargate's money in actual fact, to a widow in Leyton and a bunch of Kenyan orphans?" There was no trace of a smile now. Her gaze was steely and her voice even more clipped than usual.

"Exactly right," Andrew said, "and I'll tell you why. They've got the cash already. How do you think it will play out with the public if we ask for it back? When you want to float this company on the stock exchange, you'll have an easier ride if you can demonstrate high ethical standards. Take it from me; I've done it before."

She frowned. "If you say so. But you'd better get results from GardNet."

"I'm getting them already. You've seen the latest management report." Andrew was undaunted. He chose battles he expected to win.

"By the way," he asked boldly, "I assume you're pleased we'll be recovering £79m?"

Angie Ross had the grace to blush. She looked rather pretty, although Andrew forbore to tell her. It probably wasn't the effect she wished to achieve.

"Incidentally," Andrew said, "I think we'll have our next meeting in the Midlands."

His discussion with Ross over, Andrew glanced at his diary. The last appointment of the day was with Lucy. He'd manage it in time if he caught the next train. Carpe diem, Andrew thought. Seize the day. Stroking his beard, he checked her status on Facebook.

A smile spread across his face. "Running late," he messaged Lucy. "Want to catch up over dinner?"

Appendix A Characters

Jonathan 'Boris', a tax specialist
Melissa, a flute player and Boris's girlfriend
Szymon, a Polish concierge in Boris' apartment block
Jed, Chief Executive Officer (CEO) of GardNet
Valerie, Jed's PA
Mark, Chief Financial Officer (CFO) of GardNet
Raj, Sales Director of GardNet
Andrew, CEO of Madrigal
Ruby, Madrigal Sales and Project Manager
Helena, Mark's wife
Lucy, GardNet Human Resources Manager
Jeannie, a dating coach
Eleanor, Jed's adoptive mother
Virginia, Eleanor's younger sister
Darren, Virginia's son
Monica, Virginia's daughter
Taylor, a journalist from Ambertown, New Jersey
Annie-Belle, a teacher in Ambertown
Matthew, GardNet's communications manager
Dirk, a Dutch photographer
Dan, a Dutch photographer
Lianne, Andrew's ex-girlfriend
Marta, Szymon's wife
Adam, Andrew's lawyer
Danny, Boris' friend
Lee, Boris' friend
Diani, Lee's wife
Caroline 'Caz', a teacher and charity worker
Alexa, a violinist
Piotr, Szymon's friend
Tomasz, Szymon and Marta's young son
Anna, a Polish cleaner
Ravi, an Indian law student
Scott, a headhunter
Darryl, COO of Stargate

Angie, CFO of Stargate
Kristina, a Russian model
Lech, Szymon's friend
Andrzej, Anna's boyfriend

THANK YOU!

Thank you for reading **After The Interview** - I hope you enjoyed it! If you think your friends would like the book, please tell them about it, or even pass your copy on to them. Paperbacks are a joy worth sharing.

You can find out more about me on my website at **aaabbott.co.uk**. You'll find free short stories there too. I also review books in my blog, so if you're searching for something new to read, look no further.

You might also like my other books. The **Trail Series** begins with **The Bride's Trail.** Twenty grand is missing from Shaun Halloran's casino, and so is glamorous croupier Kat White. He plans to kill her – can her friends warn her in time? As Shaun's search moves from central London to the hidden tunnels of Birmingham's Jewellery Quarter, the stakes couldn't be higher.

The Vodka Trail sees business rivals at loggerheads – even when they're both kidnapped by terrorists and depend on each other to survive.

Latest in the series, **The Grass Trail**, focuses on an obsessive killer plotting revenge from his prison cell.

Up In Smoke, my very first book, features Big Tobacco, counterfeit cigarettes and corporate spies. It isn't just smoking that kills...

Each book is also a tale of two cities, London and Birmingham, and the tensions between them. Have fun reading them – and please let me know what you think!

AA Abbott

Lightning Source UK Ltd.
Milton Keynes UK
UKOW04f0958201017
311329UK00001B/34/P

9 780992 962104